SPELLMONKEYS

BOOK ONE

TAVERN
RATS

SPELLMONKEYS
BOOK ONE: TAVERN RATS
Copyright ©2022 by Matt Youngmark

Cover design and map also by Matt Youngmark
Back cover art by Frost Llamzon *(@FrostLlamzon)*

www.youngmark.com

CONTENTS

FOR TREVOR DOYLE

The best dungeon master
(and, more importantly, friend)
a sixteen-year-old dork could
ever hope to find

N. GLUUMWILDE

Oldbridge

Dredgehaven

1st Finger.

2nd Finger.

3rd Finger.

4th Fing.

Thumb.

6th Finger.

7th Finger.

ALTAR

BANDIT CAMP

J.

Temple of Unrelenting Evil

KRAKENS!

Arena

Burt

N.

RIVER

IMPERIAL ROAD

FOREST PATH

WATCH OUTPOST

CHAPTER ONE

INITIATIVE

I was trying to figure out where I was.

I mean, I knew where I *was*. I'd been working in the Institute Administrator's private study—a suite of three stone-walled, windowless rooms packed to the gills with arcane tomes and magical artifacts—for several hours. But I was trying to determine where the study itself was, and it had proven weirdly difficult.

As usual, I had entered the study through a peregrine gate, a truly remarkable bit of magic that created a big, circular doorway of translucent blue light. It connected the Administrator's office at the Sorcery Institute to her private residence, and even though I'd been through it dozens of times, the sheer wonder of stepping through an enchanted hole carved into thin air hadn't worn off. As far as I knew, I was the only student on campus with access to the study in the Administrator's private residence. Which, since she always arrived at work through the portal, could theoretically be anywhere. Everyone assumed she simply lived in one of Dredgehaven's nicer neighborhoods and kept the location secret to prevent random students from showing up uninvited.

A weeks-long research rabbit hole, however, had led me to a very different conclusion.

It had all started with a set of magic orbs from the Administrator's collection, each containing a pinpoint of mysterious light. The lights pressed against the edge of the glass and pointed in a fixed direction no matter how I spun them—southeast from the Sorcery Institute but, curiously, north from the study. The Administrator's records included very little about them (her cataloging system could accurately be described as "a big list,") so I had taken the orbs on as an idle research project. For three weeks, I pored through tomes, compared maps, and even hitched a ride on an oxcart out to Oldbridge and as far south as Burt, using the light inside one of the orbs to triangulate.

I had finally discovered what they were and where they pointed. And it was big. Like, 'priceless relic hidden beneath an ancient temple for centuries' big. If my calculations were correct, every time I stepped through that portal I was leaving Dredgehaven entirely and teleporting miles away to a very specific location in the middle of Gluumwilde forest.

Before I got too excited about the magical discovery of a lifetime, though, I was going to make certain that the Administrator truly lived where I thought she did. And it wasn't like I could just pop my head out to check—I only had access to the study, and the door leading to the rest of her home was quite sturdy and extremely locked. Fortunately, I had come up with an alternate means of verification.

This part was going to be fun.

Before I could get started, the peregrine gate opened with a muffled "*vorp*," and I stiffened in my chair. Although I was explicitly permitted to be there, digging into the

Administrator's secrets was surely crossing some kind of line, and even after three years at the Institute I was still medium-terrified of her. Rather than the Administrator, though, a single sheet of parchment came through the gate and floated haphazardly to the floor. That would be Uyando, the Administrator's student assistant, passing a note since he wasn't allowed to step through the gate to pester me in person. He was the latest in a string of assistants who I'd seen come and go—the truth was, most of my fellow students didn't spend more than six months at their studies before rushing out to seek their fortunes. The Sorcery Institute was, if I'm entirely honest, kind of a terrible school. But it was the only one in all the Conquered Lands that would allow a "student of significant potential" to defer tuition on the promise of future payment, which made it my only option.

Uyando and I had been close, briefly. It was a whole thing. But I was in the middle of something, and this wouldn't be the first time he called me back to school for some inconsequential matter just to get under my skin. Whatever he needed could wait.

I pulled out my map and put my finger on a blank spot in the northeastern quadrant. I had drawn a little "x" on it to mark the spot where the Administrator's residence should be. Curiously, however, every time I walked through the portal that mark disappeared, only to reappear when I returned to the Institute. There was magic at play here, and I was going to find out what kind.

I pulled a notebook from my bag, opened it to the spell I needed, and set it on the table beside the map. Then I took a pinch of dried mistletoe from a pouch on my belt, breathed deeply, and cleared my mind. The incantation was in the ancient language of the tortoise mages, but fortunately, I spoke tortoise mage pretty well.

"*Mmmguv lub qhov gnov tusmmm temmkab temmmnung.*"

I tossed the mistletoe into the air, where it was consumed in a flash of light. There were many branches of magic, but this was sorcery, which meant the magic itself was stored in a spellbook (or, in my case, a mishmash of notebooks and journals that I enchanted myself). Then a unique ritual—usually involving an incantation or hand gesture, and always including some physical component like mistletoe—would release that magic into the world. I took the briefest moment to savor it as it passed through me, flowing like a river, if that river were made entirely of very gentle, pleasant bees—

And suddenly, my nostrils exploded in pain.

Okay, I should have anticipated that. The spell was called Smell Magic, and it was used to sense the presence of magic and determine its particular nature. Every type of magic had a unique scent if you knew how to smell it—sorcery, for the record, smelled a little like dried fish. The problem was, I had cast the spell in a room stuffed with magical artifacts of every description, and now it felt as if someone had smashed the entire contents of a perfumery on my face.

Squinting through the tears, I clamped my nose shut and snatched my map off the table, bolting into an adjoining room (and smacking my shoulder squarely against the door frame in the process). Pressing my body into the emptiest corner, I managed to get most of the offending magic outside the range of my spell, but there was no time to wait for the burning to stop. I jammed the blank spot on my map up against my nose and sniffed as hard as I could. It was pungent, like overripe oranges with maybe a hint of wet dog. It was unlike any magic I'd ever smelled. Now I just needed something to compare it to.

I hurried into the third room—quickly, before the spell faded—and found what I was looking for. On a display case, inside an ornate iron cage, was what looked like a dismembered hand made of clockwork and bronze, all that remained of an ancient gnomish automaton from the Eighteenth Age. I stuck my nose in between the ironwork and inhaled. Stinky citrus dog, exactly like whatever had erased the mark from my map. I pressed my face against the rough, black stone of the chamber wall, and got a faint whiff of the same scent. That gnomish magic was in the very walls of the study.

As far as I was concerned, that proved it. The Administrator's study was, however improbably, exactly where I suspected: *the legendary hidden gnomish city of Jülskegnom.* I mean, the city wasn't that big of a secret—it appeared on several of the older maps in the Institute library. But it was surrounded by miles of dense forest, and enchanted so that it would disappear from any map that came near it, which made it pretty hard to locate unless you knew exactly where to look.

This meant that I was standing somewhere in a legendary, hidden city at that very moment. And what's more, it verified the rest of my research, which meant that nearby, buried beneath an ancient, forbidden temple—

I heard the subtle, familiar *vorp* from the other room and poked my head out the door (my spell had faded, sparing my nasal passages further assault). The gate had already closed, but another note was settling on the floor. In fact, it was a third note, the second having come at some point during my olfactory adventure. I gathered them up to find that they all carried the same message, written in Uyando's increasingly irritated hand:

Your presence is required in the office of the Institute Administrator.

The gate opened yet again, and closed immediately after a much smaller scrap of parchment popped out of it. I could read the single word inscribed on it as it floated to the floor.

NOW.

Then, in a steady rhythm, came four more portals and four more messages. *Vorp. Vorp. Vorp. Vorp.* NOW. NOW. NOW. NOW—

On the fourth *vorp*, I stuck my arm directly into the gate, holding it open, and stepped through.

"WHAT!?"

Uyando stumbled out of my way, a stack of parchment scraps still in his hand. To my surprise, he looked more upset than smug. In the doorway behind him stood Kuminik, the imperial watchman assigned to the Institute to deal with any nefarious activity that surpassed the scope of school discipline.

"Frinzil the Sorcery Student," he said formally. The tone was odd since we knew each other fairly well (I probably spent more time socializing with Institute staff than I did with other students, but in my defense, they were far more interesting). "I am to escort you from the premises immediately for failure to pay tuition for the past," he glanced down at the written order in his hand, "thirty-four months?"

"I… it… but…" I was so shocked that my mouth could barely form sentences. This was all a mistake! It had to be! "I have a deferred tuition!"

"If you needed money," Uyando said, "you could have asked."

I had no idea what about our relationship made him think that was true. Uyando was a high elf, and class distinctions between assorted varieties of humans eluded him, so he had treated me (initially, anyway) the same way he treated any other non-elf on campus. He was also one of the few students who actually seemed to care about learning, and we became fast friends the previous summer when he first arrived. Alas, it was barely a week before he decided our friendship could be something more than that, which immediately and permanently ruined everything.

The Sorcery Institute drew in aspiring spellcasters of all ages, but the bulk of the students were in their late teens and early twenties, which made the school a hotbed of budding sexuality. Frankly, I was baffled by all of it—the raw, physical attraction and jittery sexual energy that seemed to consume so much of my classmates' attention had always eluded me. All I knew was that if a friendship threatened to turn romantic, all the parts that were important to me—cama-raderie, shared interests, conversations long into the night about obscure bits of academia—were swept aside in favor of satisfying some primal, physical urge that I didn't even seem to have. It had happened to me more than once, although the first time was partly my own fault for wondering if I might find something with another girl that I had never found with boys.

It didn't matter. None of it mattered. The other students all came and went anyway, while I was here—

To stay. My attention snapped back to the matter at hand. "This is all a misunderstanding—Kuminik, you have to believe me."

"The law is clear," he said, holding up the written order. It had the word "EVICTION" emblazoned across the top, and "Frinzil Sorcery Student" scrawled into what appeared to be a standard form (imperial paperwork generally required more than one name—they had used "Frinzil Cooksdaughter" while I was growing up). Suddenly I had to fight off involuntary tears because I recognized the handwriting.

The Institute Administrator had written up the order herself.

"But that's not—" I blinked determinedly. "Just let me talk to the Administrator first! You're the one who's always saying there's a difference between law and justice—if this is all a big mistake, how can that be justice?"

Kuminik was from Tanneghede, a country far from the shores of the Conquered Lands. Although my complexion wasn't as dark as his, and my curls wilder, I clearly shared some heritage with him, which I think is why he had always taken a liking to me. Also, I'd learned from our conversations that he worshiped Tafikuweli, the Tanneghede goddess of justice, which was why I was laying it on so thick.

His expression softened, and he turned to Uyando. "Very well. Can you summon the Administrator?"

"I, uh… of course," Uyando said. We were explicitly never to summon her unless it was a matter of utmost importance, so at least Uyando had decided this qualified. He took a ring from a wooden box on the desk, placed it on his finger, and muttered an incantation to it. What must have been only a few seconds felt like a full hour, and I realized I was holding my breath just as I heard the *vorp* of the peregrine gate opening. She was coming through the gate from her study, and my first thought, for some reason, was trying to remember how much of a mess I had left there.

"Leave us," the Administrator said, not bothering to make eye contact with Kuminik or Uyando. Or me. She dropped a stack of books on her desk. "I imagine you're here to plead your case?"

Mildly terrifying or not, I admired the Institute Administrator as much as anyone I'd ever met. She was human—Westerhelmian, to be specific—and had built the Sorcery Institute from the ground up almost single-handedly. I suppose the way she carried herself reminded me of my mother—they both exuded confidence and authority. Which explained why part of me always yearned for that moment at the end of the day when all the formality would melt away and she'd shower me with unconditional love. I mean, the Institute Administrator wasn't my mom, so of course that moment never came. The office door closed, leaving us alone, and her gaze finally turned to meet mine.

"Did I do something wrong?" It was all I could muster.

"Frinzil, do you know why we offer deferred tuition to promising students without the means to pay?" She didn't wait for a response. "It's not because we enjoy their company. It's because powerful sorcerers tend to accrue wealth. It's because, generally speaking, they're good for it." Her tone wasn't castigating. It was simply the matter-of-fact way she explained things when she didn't particularly care if the person understood or not, and hearing her use it on me was devastating.

"And yet we're coming up on three years, and it appears that you haven't formed any plan whatsoever to pay us back."

I *had* formed a plan. It was to make myself so useful that I practically became part of the staff, and when an official position opened up maybe they'd hire me for it, and then I could continue studying magic forever. I mean, it wasn't a great plan. And maybe I had been a fool for thinking it was working, but this was the first time since my admission interview almost three years ago that anyone had even mentioned tuition. Part of the reason I was so hurt was that I was blindsided, as if the Administrator didn't even care enough to warn me ahead of time that it might come to this.

"I... I do so much to help out—" I started.

"Which has not gone unnoticed," she said, cutting me off as she slid into her chair and began leafing through a tome. "Professor Grimgaffler, in particular, has grown quite accustomed to foisting his duties upon you. He's gone so far as to call you 'indispensable,' which is why I allowed this to go on as long as it has. And yet when I asked him if I could take your tuition out of his salary," she raised her eyes to meet mine, "suddenly your dispensability was reassessed."

"What if..." The tears were coming back. "What if I start paying now?"

"Frinzil, I could have had five students come and go in the time you've been here," she said cooly. "Do you have five full tuitions at your disposal?" She knew I didn't. The very idea of me coming up with that kind of money was absurd.

"I can get it!" I insisted.

Maybe, just maybe, I saw the tiniest hint of a reassuring smile touch the corner of her mouth. "Very well," she said. "You have a week."

I knew better than to push back. So for some reason I bowed—bowing was not something I'd seen anyone do during my time there and I regretted it instantly—and left her office in a daze. My entire world was crumbling. Without my studies, what was left? I had come to the Institute when I was nineteen, and my time working in the manor alongside my parents before that had already established that life as a domestic servant would make me miserable. But short of stumbling across literal buried treasure, how could I possibly—

Wait. *Literal. Buried. Treasure.*

I knew what I had to do.

NOTES FROM HENK THE BARD:

Frinzil: FRIN-zle.

Uyando: oo-YAN-doe.

Jülskegnom: *JOOL-skeg-NOM.*

Kuminik: KOO-min-ick.

The Institute Administrator's actual name was Argath Carnethoine, but you don't have to worry about the pronunciation because Frinzil never heard a single person use it and wasn't sure how to pronounce it herself.

The official purpose of Frinzil's visits to the study were to convert the Administrator's list into a functional catalog system, but it was taking longer than anticipated because she kept getting distracted by all the neat stuff. Also, several items on the list appeared to be missing entirely, which made her less than eager to finish the work and report her findings.

"Mmmmguv lub qhov gnov tusmmm temmkab temmmnung" translates literally into "my nostril slits inhale the mysteries of the universe," which sounds more impressive in the original tortoise mage. The tortoise mages straight-up invented sorcery so all of the incantations were in their language (which means there's plenty more impenetrable gobbledygook on the way. Just to warn you in advance).

Since this text has been translated from imperial common, you may wonder why I use phrases and speech patterns that are not native to that tongue. To which I reply: A) The familiar idioms I've chosen more accurately reflect authorial intent than a literal translation would, B) Unless you spend a lot of time conversing in imperial common, the way you *expect* the language to sound is just as made-up anyway, and C) when YOU have to share your body with an immortal smoke monster who taps into residual magic and gives you flashes of a writer's ACTUAL THOUGHTS then you can be in charge of translation, but until then MAYBE JUST SHUT UP ABOUT IT.

RANDOM ENCOUNTERS

The Crumpled Buckler was an adventurer's tavern. Not by choice, I don't think—I assumed it had opened within stumbling distance of the Sorcery Institute specifically to cater to students. But that also put it on the edge of town that bordered the broad expanse of Gluumwilde Forest, which meant a steady flow of spellcasters, sellswords, and scoundrels poured straight in from the wilderness.

Adventuring was big business in Dredgehaven. The term was essentially a euphemism for all sorts of unseemly activity, including looting ancient ruins, the wholesale slaughtering of wildlife, and sporadic battles to the death (more often than not with other adventurers). The Conquered Lands were a vast landmass that could either be classified as an enormous island or a tiny continent, and fully twenty-two distinct civilizations had ruled it over the past thousand years. Immense sections of wilderness remained uncharted by the current regime, with ancient temples literally stacked on ancient temples, which meant a vast, dense forest like Gluumwild was more or less an adventurer's paradise.

Even after sundown, the tavern was busy and well-lit (magical lighting was cheap, especially in a town with as many fledgling sorcerers as Dredgehaven). It was the first time I had ever set foot inside the place, but it certainly lived up to its reputation. Humans of every creed and nationality rubbed shoulders with a smattering of elves, an entire table full of dwarves, several orcs, at least two lizardfolk, and one mysterious figure in the corner wrapped from head to toe in gauze who might have been a troglodyte.

The table closest to me harbored a cheerful-looking assortment of strapping, blond humans surrounded by piles of discarded fur outerwear. But when they spontaneously launched into a chorus of "South Nortenheim for Nort'men," I decided to keep my distance. I started making my way toward the bar but stopped in my tracks when the hulking bartender, his face a road map of scar tissue, met my eyes with a menacing glare. Of course, I didn't have the coin to spare for a drink anyway, and even if I did, I'd be better off keeping my wits about me.

A gathering crowd at the far end of the room drew my attention. Looking closer, I recognized several of the people milling about as fellow students, but I wasn't eager to engage. Not because they were particularly awful—they were *fine*. But they already knew how awkward I was at social interaction in general, which only made the problem worse. So I did what I normally did in crowds—seek out someone who looked as uncomfortable as I was and nervously attempt small talk. I spotted an orc hovering nearby who looked like he was ready to bolt at any moment.

"Excuse me," I said in imperial common (a lot of orcs in the Conquered Lands didn't speak orcish, and I didn't want to presume). "Do you happen to know what all those people are gathered for?"

The orc jumped, startled. He was about my age and half a head shorter than me but at least twice as broad, with the kind of physique that came from carrying heavy things for a living. A fight-or-flight response played across his face, and although it finally settled on *speak*, his posture made it clear that he was keeping the first two options open.

"Old man dead," he grunted. He squinted one eye and just stared at me as if that explained everything.

For the life of me, I had no idea why anyone would gather around to see an *old dead man*. He had spoken with a thick orcish accent, though, and one that was unfamiliar to me. Which could mean he was what people called a "wild orc" from one of the independent tribes that roved the Conquered Lands avoiding contact with civilization. I had about a million questions, but it felt rude to pry, so I tried to play it cool.

"Would you prefer to speak in orcish?" I asked, switching to his native tongue. Imperial common had only served as the official language in these parts for a couple of generations, and plenty of folks still didn't speak it at all.

His face lit up. "Yes! It's so nice to—wait, what?" He made an almost exaggerated appraisal of my decidedly human features. Orcs didn't have a written language, which made non-native speakers all the rarer. "Where did you learn orcish?"

"Oh, my parents were orcs." I realized this would do very little to remedy his confusion. "I mean, technically I guess they were muddledfolk like me, but orcs pretty much raised me."

Several of the continent's previous conquerors were human civilizations, and muddledfolk were descended from all of them (humans were renowned for the enthusiasm with which they interbred). We'd been here far longer than the Westerhelm Empire had, or the goblins before them, or the harpies before them. In a way, we were the closest thing the Conquered Lands had to a native population. My birth mother had scrubbed floors in an imperial manor but fled immediately after childbirth, so the orcish couple who worked as butler and cook—my *real* parents—raised me as their own. My mom was the wisest person I'd ever known, and my dad was the kindest, so I'd unquestionably lucked out in that department.

"I'm Frinzil," I said, extending a hand.

It was as if a dam had burst. "Brukkthog!" the orc beamed, grabbing my hand and shaking it with enthusiasm. "You can call me Brukk, though, if you want. Yeah, the old man was a spellcaster. Like, for an adventuring party?" His voice grew a bit more somber. "Krakenfire got him. He was with them for a couple years—longer than most, I guess. Ashes aren't even cold, and they're already holding tryouts for the next one."

I made my way through the crowd to get a better view, and my new friend followed. Brukk, who must have spent a great deal of time at the Crumpled Buckler based on how much he knew about the regulars, filled me in on the party as we watched the scene unfold.

Adventurers came in all varieties, but this group was right out of Adventuring 101 (and I should know since I sometimes *taught* Adventuring 101 when Professor Grimgaffler couldn't make it to class). They had a warrior to focus on stabbing things, a pathfinder to navigate the wilds, a priest to administer healing when the stabbing didn't go well, and a scoundrel to pick locks,

spring traps, and such. These were clearly seasoned profession-
als, and all they were missing was a caster (I felt bad for their
departed companion, but to be honest, his timing couldn't be
better) which meant that I could slot right in. They were perfect.
I could barely believe my good fortune.

The only hurdle, of course, was the crowd of aspiring
applicants already lined up ahead of me for the job.

The group's pathfinder—a broad-shouldered, hirsute human
who I assume was called Wülf ironically since he obviously
suffered from lycanthropy—appeared to be running the
auditions. And the sorcery student standing before him (I think
his name was Edmund, or possibly Eglund) looked thoroughly
crestfallen.

Wülf pushed his chair back with a loud, wooden scrape,
and stood. "Enough!" he said to the room in general. "Who
else is a recent graduate of that magic school up the hill?" About
a dozen people raised their hands (at least half of which were
lying, since I knew for a fact they had yet to graduate).

"Go," Wülf said definitively. "We don't want you. Take your
four cantrips and single, crappy field spell and seek
employment elsewhere."

With a general groan of dejection, the crowd dispersed.
Okay, that didn't bode well.

"See, this is why you don't look for casters in Dredgehaven,"
the priestess said. She was a human of Omaki descent called
Sohyun, although judging by her regalia she worshiped a
Nortenhemian goddess. "I heard Spencimus is holed up over
in Oldbridge."

The party's scoundrel was a scary-looking deep elf named
Verexis, who also appeared to be their leader. She spat on the
floor. "Ugh, that guy's the worst. Plus, he demands one and a

quarter shares, which makes accounting a pain in my ass." She cast her eyes around the room with little enthusiasm. "What else is on hand?"

Of the original crowd, only two applicants remained. The first was a human druid (you could always spot a druid because there was a druidic spell that magically wove a cloak from available foliage—druids wore them almost exclusively, partly because it helped them feel connected to nature, and partly because, hey, free cloak). As he approached, Verexis produced a shard of glowing crystal hanging from a chain and kept her eyes fixed on it.

I recognized the magic. It was an amulet of truth—or a piece of one, at least. The Institute administrator had such an amulet in her collection, a relic of immense power that would peer deep into your soul and draw out truths that even you didn't know were there. I'd had one previous experience with it, and can tell you that the process was not pleasant. A shard like this wouldn't have nearly as much power, but it would glow brightly if a statement was true and turn black if the speaker uttered anything they knew in their heart to be a lie.

The poor druid, alas, didn't stand a chance. Druidic magic is drawn directly from nature rather than bound up in books and incantations the way sorcery was. As a result, the spirits that channeled it tended to pull druids steadily away from the civilized world. Most were lost to the wilds eventually, and with his unwashed beard and crusty, shoeless feet, it didn't take an amulet of truth to see that this one was well on his way to that end.

The druid stated his name (Sprig), his school of magic (druidism), and when asked why he wanted to join their party, began to praise the virtues of city life, which he knew all about because he definitely lived in one, and not under a bush outside town. Verexis's crystal didn't glimmer once after the word "druidism," and he was summarily dismissed.

"Next!" Wülf bellowed.

The druid shuffled off and was replaced by an elvish woman in a scarlet robe, her blue skin so pale it could have been the moon in the middle of Verexis's midnight sky. After the elves first held dominion over the Conquered Lands, they had split into two groups, one living in cities high in the mountains and the other in caverns deep underground. Reliable elvish history was hard to come by, so I didn't know much about the particulars, but there were undoubtedly longstanding cultural animosities between the two groups. The pair of them locked eyes and scowled at each other as if competing for the title of Most Terrifying Elf.

Wülf finally broke the silence. "Name and school of magic?"

"A'maelote," she said. "Witchcraft."

That seemed to give him pause. "Okay. And, uh, why do you want to join our group?"

The pale elf raised an eyebrow, either considering the question or deciding how to punish the impudent fool dumb enough to ask it. When she finally spoke, it was in a voice devoid of any hint of emotion.

"The Dark Lord requires souls to fuel his infernal machinations."

Wülf's eyes darted to the crystal, which was shining bright. "Next!"

The elf glared at him, then turned to glare at *me* and walked away backward, slowly, without breaking eye contact. It was extremely unsettling. She was right, though—I appeared to be the only applicant left. I gathered my wits as Wülf looked at me expectantly (to be clear, it was a look that said he wasn't expecting much).

"Name?" he asked. "School of magic?" As I was about to speak, I felt a gentle hand on my shoulder, and a short, broad form stepped out from behind me.

"Brukkthog," my orc friend said, planting his feet and setting his jaw, which trembled slightly nevertheless.

"Summoner."

NOTES FROM HENK THE BARD:

Brukkthog: BRUCK-thog

Wülf: WOLF

Sohyun: so-YOON

Verexis: vuh-REX-iss

Spencimus: SPENCE-ih-muss

Sprig: SPRIG

A'maelote: ah-MAY-loat

Adventuring had become so prominent in Dredgehaven that in recent years it had even supplanted pulling random things out of the river as the town's primary economic engine.

Nortenheim had ruled the Conquered Lands during the Sixteenth Age, and their descendants considered it to be their ancestral home. They weren't alone in this, of course—a lot of people claimed the Conquered Lands as their ancestral home. In fact, the song "South Nortenheim for Nort'men" was adapted directly from the much older "Omaki ki, Omaki wuhai." It lost a considerable amount of charm in translation.

Encountering an Omaki priestess who worshiped a Nortenhaim goddess was not as uncommon as you might think. The multitudinous cultures of the Conquered Lands formed less of a melting pot and more of a stew, thick with distinct ingredients and unexpected flavor combinations.

The joke about the Twenty-Second Age, of course, was that it was expected to last about twenty seconds, even though Westerhelm rule had endured for a good four decades and at that point seemed fairly stable. The many and varied ages of the Conquered Lands, up until then: **I)** Dragons. **II)** Tortoise mages. **III)** Lich kings. **IV)** Elves. **V)** Dwarves. **VI)** Dwarves, aquatic. **VII)** Giants. **VIII)** Werewolves. **IX)** Humans, Omaki. **IXb)** Ghosts (not considered an official age for reasons that can only be chalked up to historian ghost-racism). **X)** Centaurs. **XI)** Humans, Tannehgede. **XII)** Bugbears (very briefly). **XIII)** Elves again. **XIV)** Lizardfolk (no relation to tortoise mages). **XV)** Elves for the third time. **XVI)** Humans, Nortenheimish. **XVII)** Gnomes commanding automaton army. **XVIII)** Gnomish automaton army, uprising. **XIX)** Kobolds. **XX)** Harpies. **XXI)** Hobgoblin/regular goblin alliance. **XXII)** Humans, Westerhelmian.

CHAPTER THREE

PARTY SPLIT

The mysteries of Brukk's background had already sparked my curiosity, and now it was blazing like a grease fire. In all my studies, I had never heard of an orc who practiced magic. Although if he was going to study magic, summoning made perfect sense, because the practices were never committed to paper, only taught directly from master to apprentice. Most people didn't know this, but the reason orcs didn't have a written language was that their eyes didn't work the way human eyes did. There was a spell that let you see like an orc, and it's hard to explain, but orcish vision bathed the world in an explosion of color that varied based on proximity, temperature, texture, and several other factors. It explained how my dad could look at a pot of soup and tell you it needed salt, but it also made reading a particular challenge. Unless the words were inscribed with something much thicker than ink, orcish vision made the texture of the parchment easier to distinguish than whatever was written on it.

"That's odd," Verexis said coolly, snapping my attention back to the scene playing out before me. "The old man never mentioned that he was training his lackey to do tricks."

Oh—Brukk didn't just know this group so well from seeing them around the Crumpled Buckler. He had worked for them. That actually made a lot more sense.

"Brukkthog," he repeated, his jaw quiver intensifying. "Summoner."

Verexis's lip curled in amusement. "Alright. Have at it then. Summon something," she said. "Right here. Let's see what you've got."

Expressions around the table ranged from mild curiosity to naked confusion, and the group's warrior—a half-orc named Krogos who had yet to venture a single word in my presence— glared at Brukk with open contempt. Brukk cleared his throat, gulped, and pushed a heavy wooden chair away from the table, somehow even more loudly than when Wülf had done it earlier. Now I was wholly engrossed. Comparative magic was one of my favorite areas of study, but I had never witnessed an actual summoning.

Brukk pricked his finger with a steak knife and traced a circle roughly the diameter of his forearm on the table's surface. Very little blood dribbled from the cut, but he proceeded to add invisible, scribbly details to the inscription, all while keeping his eyes screwed shut.

As soon as he finished, the shape of an arcane, somewhat lopsided circle flashed briefly on the table, and a puff of malodorous smoke materialized, quickly dissipating to reveal a small creature. Its tail was ragged, its fur patchy, and putrid yellow pus was caked in its beady eyes.

"Hragma's Holy Hammer," Sohyun swore, aghast. "Is that a zombie squirrel?"

Wülf looked equally befuddled. "Why would you summon a *zombie* squirrel? Anything you would possibly need it for could be accomplished more deftly by a *regular* squirrel."

Brukk looked as surprised as either of them. "It not supposed be zombie," he said. He stared at the thing for a moment before continuing the ritual. "Um, by blood seal, by ancient power tradition, Brukkthog bind squirrel to—"

With a screech, the thing leaped directly onto Brukk's body, scurrying around his torso. "Get it off me, get it off!" he squealed, in orcish this time, turning backward in a circle and pawing frantically at his shoulders in a desperate attempt to reach the small of his back.

Laughter erupted around the table. From what I knew, the power of a summoner mostly boiled down to strength of will, and Brukk had just lost a battle of wills with a dead rodent.

"Your services won't be needed here," Verexis said.

The squirrel hopped off Brukk and scampered haphazardly out of sight. His face fell, and I saw his shoulders shaking as he turned his back to leave. Part of me wanted to follow him and make sure he was okay, but it would have to wait.

"I have no idea what that even was," Wülf said, "but *next*, I guess." He turned to me. "Did you want to state your name and school of magic, or can I get back to drinking?"

I was completely thrown by what I had just seen. "Frinzil!" I blurted. It sounded way too eager when I heard it come out of my mouth. "Uh, sorcery."

"Yeah," Wülf said. "You wouldn't happen to be from that school, would you? The one I said I didn't want to see anyone from? Ever?"

Verexis was flagging down a server with one hand, but holding her crystal up in plain view with the other. She needn't have bothered. I generally stuck to the truth as a matter of principle, mostly because I was a horrendous liar.

"I am," I said plainly. "But I'm not like the other students."

The crystal glowed. "Apparently not," Wülf said. "Okay, how many spells have you got?"

"Twenty-nine."

The gem continued to glow, bright and steady, and the priestess let out a small gasp.

"Twenty-nine?" Verexis asked. Now I had her attention. "Hot damn, which ones?"

I couldn't help but smile, despite myself. The Institute might exist mostly to churn out cookie-cutter sorcerers who wanted nothing more from life than to fight monsters and loot temples, but you could still learn quite a lot there if you set your mind to it. And over the past three years, I had most assuredly done so.

"Magical Stamp," I said, beginning the list. "Smell Magic, Ghostly Hand, Cause Minor Wounds . . ."

"Sure, the four cantrips that literally every boy wizard learns at wizard college," Wülf said. "What else?"

"Resist Hunger," I continued proudly. "Resist Itch, Resist *Loneliness*, Eyes of the Orc—"

"Eyes of the Orc?" Wülf sounded genuinely baffled. "Why? Orcs can't read. If you cast it, you wouldn't be able to cast anything else until it wore off."

"Well, it might not be very useful in the field," I said. "But have you ever looked at a pot of soup from the perspective of—"

"Uh-huh. What else?"

"Um, Disguise Small Item?" Now I was off my rhythm. "Irritating Lights?"

This time it was Verexis who interrupted. "Wait, are all twenty-nine of these spells cantrips?"

"Are there even twenty-nine cantrips?" Sohyun asked.

Cantrips were the most basic sorcery spells, requiring very little magical energy to cast. There were, in fact, thirty of them in known magical lore. I had mastered all but one—Gust of Smell, since one of its components was ground dragonscale, and even if I could afford ground dragonscale, I can't imagine wasting it on Gust of Smell.

"Don't underestimate cantrips," I insisted. "Under the right circumstances…"

This time the laughter was nothing short of uproarious. "Twenty-nine cantrips!" Wülf chuckled, wiping his eyes. "That's the best thing I've ever heard."

I genuinely couldn't tell if he meant it as a compliment. "So… am I in?"

"What? Of course not." He looked around the room. "Is that everyone? Are we done here?"

I realized I had let this entire evening completely get away from me. "Wait!" I said. "I'm not trying to join your party—not permanently, anyway. I came here to hire you! I have a quest."

"Yeah," Wülf said. "We're actually pretty set for those, too."

"But it's a really good one!"

Verexis glanced at her crystal, which was still glowing steadily, and sighed with what I can only describe as exasperation. "Fine," she said. "Let's hear about this really good quest."

By this point, I was good and flustered, but there was nothing for it. I pulled the map from my bag and spread it out on the table. It didn't unfurl quite as majestically as I'd hoped because it was a relatively small map, but what it lacked in size, it made up for with accuracy.

"Hidden in the forest of Gluumwilde," I began, "not two days' march from this very tavern, lies a forgotten kobold temple from the Nineteenth Age…"

"You mean the Temple of Unrelenting Evil?" Wülf interrupted. "Let me stop you right there."

"You know about the Temple of Unrelenting Evil?"

"Yeah, it's right on a main trail." He tapped the map with one finger, and sure enough, there was a line I had dotted with my own hand representing a forest path. "We spent a couple of days there back in 36, and it was pretty much picked clean even back then."

"There's a hidden chamber, though," I said.

Verexis scoffed. "Are you suggesting that I can't find a hidden chamber? Get your own party." She gestured vaguely toward the bar. "Try the sad druid."

None of this was going the way I had imagined it. "I'm not casting aspersions on your… scoundreling," I insisted. The crystal was still glowing, so at least she knew I was sincere. "The treasure isn't inside the temple, it's beneath it—the whole thing was built on top of ancient ruins. *Second Age* ruins."

The crystal verified my statement, but Verexis didn't seem persuaded. "Maybe you believe it's there, but I still think you're full of it. If this treasure of yours is so well hidden, buried for—what, a thousand years?—how did *you* find out about it?"

Now my confidence was shot entirely. Fortunately, I had spent most of the afternoon rehearsing my speech, and soldiered on.

"Snippets of legend cobbled together from multiple texts…" The crystal flickered, and I became highly aware that every word I spoke was being scrutinized for accuracy. Did I sound too pretentious? Would the crystal pick up on tone? "Uh, hidden to all but the cleverest…" Wait, now it sounded boastful. What was the crystal's policy on bragging? "I mean, it's not like it takes a genius to cross-reference them…"

The crystal dimmed. To be honest, I did believe I was something of a genius at cross-referencing.

"Books!" I blurted at last, closing my eyes and rubbing my temples, utterly defeated. "I found it by reading books."

"Second Age," Wülf muttered. "That's tortoise mage stuff. What do you think is in there?"

I peeled one eye open and found the entire party looking at me thoughtfully. I wasn't at all eager to tip my hand because it was the sort of treasure some people would kill for. That crystal was glowing at me threateningly, though, so it wasn't like I could lie.

"Something the tortoise mages never wanted to be found," I said carefully. "I can't know for certain what it is."

The crystal flickered between blue and black. "Maybe not for certain," Verexis said, "but you have a pretty good idea. Spill."

"A spell scroll," I said deliberately, trying as hard as I could to focus on the truth of my statement rather than the part I was leaving out. "Original grimoire. Category seven."

"That's the highest category," Sohyun said, sounding impressed. "And sorcery scrolls—anyone can cast those things." She was right. The entire point of a spell scroll was that the magic had already flowed through a sorcerer into the parchment, so even someone with no magical training could provide the components and incantation to finish the job.

"That'd be worth snatching up even if we weren't going to sell it, just to use ourselves," Wülf said. He turned to Verexis. "What do you think?"

"The Temple of Unrelenting Evil is pretty much on the way to the kraken's nest," she said. "We could grab the scroll along the way and still make it in plenty of time. Krogos?"

All three of them turned toward the warrior, who had yet to speak the entire time I'd been there. Now he rubbed his stubbled chin slowly, carefully considering his words.

"Fuck it," he said in a voice like obsidian gravel. "I got time for the Temple of Unrelenting Evil."

I could hardly believe my ears. *It was happening.*

"Now if we could only rustle up a goddamned spellmonkey," Verexis said, "we'd be ready to go."

"Spellmonkey" was a disparaging term for any type of magician, since casters had a reputation for being the most difficult to work with of the standard adventuring party roles. The joke was that a monkey trained to cast Dome of Burning would be ideal, but until such a creature could be found, some other magic-wielder would have to suffice.

"Um, I think you may have misunderstood," I said. "It's my quest. I'm the monkey."

They ignored me completely. "So what do we do?" Wülf asked. "Revisit the demon elf? Head for Oldbridge?"

Verexis groaned and surveyed the room, her eyes very pointedly not settling on me. "I guess we're out of alternatives. Oldbridge it is."

I tried to muster an argument, but the only thing that emerged from my mouth was the word "but," repeated several times in a steady rhythm.

"Thanks for the tip, Cantrips," Wülf said, setting down a small stack of coins to pay for their meal and flipping another across the table toward me. "That one's your finder's fee. You keep up those studies, okay?"

With that, they were gone.

I fell into a chair at the now-empty table in shock. They stole my quest. Were they allowed to steal my quest? I just couldn't wrap my brain around it.

I have no idea how long I sat in silence, but eventually a shadow fell over me, and I looked up to find the mountainous barkeep looming. "Don't pay that lot any mind," he said. "Hey, we keep a basement stocked with rats if you want to get some training in. Plenty of adventurers hone their skills killing rats. There's no shame in it."

I didn't *want* to hone my skills killing rats. I wanted to recover the scroll, sell it for tuition money, return to the Sorcery Institute, and never set foot outside its grounds again.

The barkeep turned to address the seat next to me, and I discovered that at some point, Brukk had joined me at the table. "Basement full of rats? No? Well, I'll tell you what, the first round's on me." He set down two tankards of thin, beige brew. "And forget about those rotters. You don't need them, anyway."

Although I had grown up among the lower rungs of an absurdly rigid class system, my parents had always taught me that optimism was a choice, and any particular challenge was only impossible until I decided it wasn't. Then again, I had never worked quite so hard for something, only to see it crushed so thoroughly and decisively to dust right before my eyes.

Unless, of course, I decided it wasn't.

The veteran adventuring party had skills and experience that put mine to shame. They also had a head start. But they still had to find the scroll, and ancient treasures didn't stay buried for centuries because they were right out in the open. I happened to have a little something up my sleeve—literally, in a pouch strapped to my arm underneath my loose-fitting robe—that would give me an edge in that department. I took a sip of ale. It tasted awful but went down surprisingly smooth and left a warm tingle in my belly, which I could only assume was why my classmates were so fond of the stuff.

I took a second drink from my tankard, this one long and steady. It might have been two parts unwarranted optimism and one part moderately-tolerable ale, but I was beginning to hatch a plan.

NOTES FROM HENK THE BARD:

Krogos: CROW-gose

Being a half-orc meant one of Krogos's parents was an orc and the other one was human. The other part of a half-anything was always human because humans were the only people who could successfully (and, remember, enthusiastically) produce offspring by copulating outside their species. Alas, such offspring was typically sterile, which was the only reason the muddledfolk population wasn't blessed with orc tusks, elf ears, centaur hooves, harpy wings, or any of the other really cool physical characteristics that non-humans brought to the table.

By "36," Wülf meant the year W.E. 36, or 36 years into the Westerhelmian Era. Serious discussion of any event more than a few decades past was almost impossible in the Conquered Lands, because nobody could agree on how the years should be numbered.

In truth, the stuff Frinzil's classmates were so fond of was significantly more expensive, but they would also drink the house ale—which the locals affectionately called "rat piss"—in a pinch.

CHAPTER FOUR

ATTACK OF
OPPORTUNITY

The sensation of waking up with my face pressed against the cover of a book was hardly new. In fact, as I drifted toward consciousness, I fully expected to find myself slumped over a table in the Institute library. That wouldn't explain the sharp pain behind one of my shoulders, though, or the dull stinging on both kneecaps. And it definitely wouldn't explain the nausea. I pried my eyes open and realized that I wasn't gently caressing my copy of *Rimbauld's Complete History of the Conquered Lands, Volume III.*

I was grinding the book into a patch of dried leaves with my face.

I bolted upright and received multiple scratches from low branches for my effort. I was in the dirt, under a tree, on the edge of what appeared to be a small forest clearing. The sunlight filtering aggressively through the overhead canopy was so painful I could only open my eyes to a squint, and in short bursts.

All memory of the previous night was hazy, but I could recall a commiseration with Brukk that grew into boisterous camaraderie as the night wore on, and round after round of tavern swill appeared as if by magic. Also... the hapless, shoe-less druid leading us through the woods to his campsite? After we were thrown out for some reason? A tavern wouldn't keep serving you drinks once you were too drunk to know if you could afford them, would they? It seemed unethical.

"How could you have forty pounds of books in here but not a single scrap of breakfast?"

I craned my neck to squint around the tree trunk and saw the terrifying elven witch rummaging through my pack. "Is this a ledger? For a barrel-making business? Why do you even have this?"

The trickle of memories burst into a flood. Now I distinctly remembered drinking more alcohol than I had consumed in all my twenty-two years combined (three tankards full, at least), declaring that the veteran adventurers who had stolen my quest were, in fact, *stupid*, and proceeding to hire an adventuring party of my own.

Brukk emerged from the underbrush, looking nothing less than chipper—the orc apparently handled his ale considerably better than I did. "Pathfinder job get food," he said in common. His arms clutched an assortment of branches and other flora. "Wülf always do moss, but it never... purpley so much. Where druid?"

The witch—her name was Mae, I remembered, which was definitely short for something, though I couldn't remember what—examined Brukk's bounty and scoffed. "I'm not eating that. The subject of meals wasn't specified in our contract, but I assume they'll be provided."

Meals? Contract? Uh-oh. "This might, uh... be a good time to go over those details again?"

Mae's stare was uncomfortably intense, and she adopted the same unflinching tone she had used the previous night. "The terms of our contract were succinct. I am to rain down fire on our enemies in exchange for one quarter share of all treasure, plus the immortal souls of any vanquished enemies or collateral damage."

Aaaaaagh.

"Did I hire you to be the party's... *warrior*?" I asked, inadvertently dropping the pretense that I had any idea what was going on. Much of what I was piecing together of the previous night's activity didn't make a lot of sense in the harsh morning light.

"You said that with the right mix of spellcasters, we, and I quote, 'wouldn't even need a warrior.'"

Okay, that part did sound like me. I had a longstanding theory that, since the various schools of magic were so diverse, a sufficiently trained caster could step in and do the job of any other party member. Of course, the words 'sufficiently trained' were doing a lot of work in that sentence.

"Brukk half pathfinder, half not-Brukk, plus backup," the orc said helpfully.

I stared at him for a moment but was completely unable to parse it. "Maybe try that again in orcish?"

"Oh! Right! I just thought it would be polite to speak a language we all knew so nobody thought I was getting, I don't know, special treatment? Because we're friends?"

My head was throbbing, and as much as I appreciated his enthusiasm, his overall perkiness cut like a knife. "Just—what was the thing you were saying before about being a pathfinder?"

He beamed. "I'll use all my knowledge from hands-on adventuring to handle as many pathfinder duties as I can. Plus summon different creatures to help with everyone else's job, too."

I remembered that he had been employed by our rivals, which meant he should have plenty of insight into the ins and outs of adventuring in general, and their group specifically. I liked the idea of that.

"I have a quarter share, too," Brukk continued. "but I didn't hear anything about souls."

"Enough with the orc noises," Mae said. "What's he saying?"

Brukk stuck his chin out. "If elf get souls, Brukk want souls, too."

Mae appeared to take this as a challenge. Her expression didn't change, but she must have adjusted her posture because now she was looming.

"If you hope to claim any shred of the bounty that has been promised to my demon lord, I absolutely recommend you kill me in my sleep. Because if I see you coming, your own soul is the only one you need worry about."

I groaned. The thing to understand about souls was that the word itself was merely a superstitious term for the magical energy that infused all living things. It was true that some of the... less reputable branches of magic utilized this energy, which was traditionally harvested upon death. A person's essence, though—their consciousness and memories, the core of who they were—remained in the life-less body, slowly rotting away with it. That's why, if you had enough gold to pay for a resurrection, a priest could pump new magical energy into you, from an entirely different source, and you'd still wake up as good as new. Witchcraft was often unpleasant and unseemly, to be sure, but it wasn't as if the practice was dooming anybody to eternal suffering in a pit of fire.

"Obey the Dark Lord," Mae continued, "or be doomed to eternal suffering *in the pits of fire.*"

Granted, its practitioners might have their own perspectives on the matter. Demon lords bestowed witch magic in much the same way gods bestowed priest magic, and as far as I could tell, the difference between the two mostly came down to public relations. I was far more worried about Mae's ambitions—and the lengths she might go to achieve them—than I was about the nature of her magic.

"Ugh. Mmmng grg hrrrrm."

The noise came from a nearby bush. A pair of legs stuck out from underneath it, bare to the thighs (above which, blessedly, remained covered by a filthy robe).

"Druid!" Brukk shouted (so loudly), using this new development as an excuse to beat a hasty retreat from his confrontation with Mae. "Druid! Any of this food?" He poked at one of the exposed legs with a branch from his breakfast collection but failed to get a response.

The druidic tradition included quite a bit of healing magic, which was most of what adventuring parties needed a priest for, so I must have hired the druid to be our party's healer. And his bond with nature would surely help shore up any gaps in Brukk's pathfinding abilities as well. So that meant I had a makeshift witch-warrior, a cobbled-together pathfinder, and a theoretical priest, pending conscious verification. Between the four of us, we had spellcasting duties more than covered. All I was missing was a scoundrel—I remember vaguely thinking that Brukk could summon something for scoundreling purposes if need be? If everything went as planned, though, the only thing we might need a scoundrel for was finding the secret chamber beneath the Temple of Unrelenting Evil.

And I already had that part taken care of.

Mae had moved on from my bag and was now sifting through Brukk's things. "The orc's been holding out," she said. "Offering leaf breakfast when he has perfectly serviceable rations in here?" She nibbled on something from one of his packs and promptly spat it out. "Puh! I take it back, all this food is disgusting. And it's barely enough for two days—less if the druid ever wakes up."

"Oh!" Brukk said. "That reminds me!" He ran toward the spot where his packs were piled up, puffing himself up like a cat and hissing at Mae until she took two bewildered steps backward. After some quick rummaging, he came bounding back with a massive leather tome.

"You like books, right? This is for you."

It was a spellbook. And a particularly expensive-looking one at that—ornately embossed, detailed with what looked like gold but was actually a compound made from baobab root, which had magical properties. It might have been the most beautiful object I had ever seen in my life. As gorgeous as it was, though, another wizard's spellbook was useless to me.

"I'm honored," I said—I genuinely was—"but, unfortunately, I can't use this. Every sorcerer's spellbook is inscribed with the name of its owner, and no one else can read it." This was probably the only thing that kept the wizarding world from descending into a chaotic, winner-take-all murder spree, to be honest.

I opened the book to check the inscription but found it blank. It was unmarked. The entire book was empty, just waiting to be filled with spells by the first sorcerer to get her hands on it. You could generally judge a spellbook by its cover, too—with binding this fancy, the enchantment would probably be powerful enough to hold every spell in the lore.

I swallowed hard. "Brukk, do you have any idea how valuable this is? I can't accept it. It's too much." The truth was, I wanted that book so badly that my hands were starting to go numb.

"It was the old man's," he said. "He wasn't… kind to me. I don't need a token to remember him by." If Brukk's teacher had been a summoner, what was he doing with a sorcerer's spellbook? It did explain why he hadn't inscribed it, though.

"Look, nobody ever thought I could be a summoner," Brukk continued. "But you came along and just accepted it. Treated me like I was a real caster, even hired me for a party of only casters…" His brow was starting to quiver now.

I placed the book back in his hands gently. "I'll tell you what. Once we find a reputable dealer, you can sell it and buy me a regular spellbook. At a fifth the cost."

"Ugh—if you two are finished talking orc and braiding each other's hair," Mae said, "should we maybe get going? Also, I'm still waiting on breakfast."

I looked at her, then at Brukk, and the pair of still-motionless bush legs. Was I really doing this? If I was going to beat the quest thieves to the temple, I didn't exactly have time to waste looking for a different adventuring party.

"Okay," I said. "Somebody wake up… um, did either of you catch his name last night?"

"Drinky the Drunk Druid," Mae said.

"No, it was definitely something to do with plants," Brukk said. "Leafmaster? Leaf… puncher? I feel like it had the human word for leaf in it."

"Can the orc just drag him?" Mae groaned. "I feel like we were in a hurry."

"Well, yes and no," I said. "The other party does have a head start, but they're headed for Oldbridge first, which is a day's travel east on the imperial highway. If we cut south through the forest, we should beat them to the temple."

"We could beat them if we take the highway, too," Brukk said, "assuming they stop at as many pubs as they usually do along the way."

"Hmm," I said. "If we stuck to the highway we'd safe from bandits." The highway was patrolled by the imperial watch, which made it far safer than traveling through the woods.

"Bandits are the least of our worries," Brukk insisted. "Bandits are, maybe, medium-dangerous? We'll be *lucky* if we run into bandits."

"What's he saying?" Mae asked. "Is he talking about me?"

I tried to rub the headache out of my forehead. "He said that bandits are medium-dangerous," I translated. "If there are even worse waiting for us in the woods, though, all the more reason to take the highway. What are your thoughts, Mae?"

She crossed her arms. "I have zero insight into this region, its dangers, or the godforsaken wilderness in general. So if you're asking me for directions, I suppose my thoughts would be that we're well and truly fucked."

Indelicate as she was, Mae wasn't wrong. I had put this group together, and it fell to me to lead it. "We'll take the imperial road," I said with what I hoped was reassuring confidence. "It'll leave us with less time to search the temple, but we shouldn't need much time." As I spoke, I unfastened a pouch I had strapped to my arm beneath my sleeve.

"Because I came prepared with this."

"The ancient treasure-finder glow ball, or whatever," Mae said. "We know. You told us last night."

"Oh." I'd thought the moment would be something of a dramatic reveal, but apparently I had already gone over the plan during the blackout portion of the previous evening. The glow ball in question was a glass orb, about the size of an apple, covered in ornate etchings and filled with a faint green mist. A pinpoint of light fluttered around inside, continually returning to the same spot at the edge of the glass as if trying to push its way through. It was an ancient hunter spirit, created by lich kings centuries ago to locate enemy magic during the war against the tortoise mages that ushered in the Third Age. The Institute administrator had an entire collection of them, and curiosity about the orbs was what started me down the rabbit hole that led me to—

Wait. "Uh, so, last night? How much did I actually tell you about…"

"The most powerful scroll in the world that's a brand new spell and a really huge secret and don't tell anyone because like every single wizard will try to murder you for it?" Mae's delivery was utterly expressionless. "Eh, not that much."

"It SEVENTH scroll," Brukk said, sticking up for me. "Six scrolls not enough. Need seven."

"It's not… we don't have six scrolls already," I said. "The Seventh Scroll is a whole legend—it's a missing spell. There are ninety-six sorcery spells in all of magical lore, and only six of those are of the highest caliber. But some believe that the tortoise mages crafted a seventh, meant to turn the tide in their war against—"

I could see their eyes glossing over. "It's basically what Mae said. It's a big secret, nobody really knows what it does, and we probably shouldn't tell anybody about it. But all we needed to do was follow this light to the scroll and we'll be in and out of the Temple of Unrelenting Evil in no time."

"Wait, the temple of what?" Mae said.

"Well, that's what the Empire calls it. In the original kobold it was just—"

"Yeah, I don't care. But you said we were going to, and I quote, 'the mysterious, hidden gnomish city of Jülskegnom.'"

Ugh. Drunk Frinzil was a blabbermouth. "No, we don't have to go there. That's just where the woman who runs my school lives."

"In the mysterious, hidden gnomish city. Of Jülskegnom."

"She has… kind of a lot going on," I said. With everything that had happened, I hadn't really had time to sit with the fact that the Institute Administrator pretty much walked through a portal every day, kicked off her shoes and hung up her cloak in a secret gnomish city. But once I'd discovered its location (quite by accident while researching the temple—Jülskegnom wasn't a particularly well-kept secret), my cartography told me that the city was the only place her residence could possibly be located.

"That's neither here nor there, though," I continued. "The orb points to the kobold temple, which is where we'll find our treasure."

Brukk stretched out one finger like he was about to tap the glass. "It's so shiny."

"Uh… maybe let's just put this away." I had kept it close to guard against pickpockets at the tavern, but it was somewhat fragile and exceedingly old, so sleeping on it every night probably wasn't the best idea. Also, I wasn't technically supposed to leave campus with it. I wrapped the orb in a cloth and put it carefully in my pack.

The Seventh Scroll secret was out of the bag, but my party seemed to have taken it in stride. Plus, my headache had diminished, my vision was more or less back to normal, and my stomach was... well, I wasn't concerned about breakfast yet, but I did feel well enough to travel. There was an intersecting highway going south from Oldbridge, so we could walk most of the way on the safety of the roads and only have to spend maybe half a day in the forest, on the lookout for—

"Queeeeeeeeeeeeek! Queeeeeeeeek!"

A piercing cry came from somewhere outside the clearing and was promptly answered by another from the opposite direction. A voice followed the calls, raspy and shrill.

"Toss your valuables on the ground and put your hands on your heads! If nobody does anything stupid, nobody needs to get hurt."

Bandits? Nooooooo! I had already chosen the non-bandit option!

"We have you surrounded, so empty your purses—and don't hold back." The second voice came from the far side of the clearing, and sounded remarkably similar to the first.

A third voice called out from somewhere above us in the treetops. "Do what she says, all of you, unless you want an arrow to the neck."

Now I was sure of it. They weren't just similar; they were the same voice. Illusion was a subset of sorcery taught at the Institute, and Limited Ventriloquism was one of its basic spells. I'd never seen anyone specialize in the art, since there were only two real ways to make money doing it: Performing tricks onstage and waylaying gullible travelers.

A quick Smell Magic spell would tell me for sure if we were dealing with an illusionist, but did I dare cast it? Brukk already had his hands on his head. Mae stood motionless, waiting for my lead. The druid was still a pair of legs under a bush.

If this was to be my first real test of leadership, so be it. I whipped out a notebook, snatched a pinch of dried mistletoe from my belt pouch, and launched into the incantation—

Only to be immediately shot with an arrow, right in the leg. My chanting was replaced by a guttural scream.

"Take no prisoners!" A swarm of hairy, humanoid creatures, each about the size of a five-year-old, sprung from the treeline.

"Ratlandia for ratlings!"

Ratlings. They had the heads and general appearance of giant rodents, but spoke and walked upright. I didn't know much about them, but I did know that they gave birth to children in litters. Meaning that the three voices I heard belonged—in all likelihood—to identical triplets.

In my defense, anyone could have made that mistake.

I tried to get my bearings, but my mangled leg refused to support any weight, and I fell to the ground. Bandits scurried around me and swung down into the clearing from ropes—they were everywhere. Casting about for the rest of my party, I just managed to catch a glimpse of Mae as she disappeared into the forest.

"No!" Brukk yelled after her. "We can take 'em!" Then, apparently realizing that she didn't even speak that language, he switched to common. "Ratling least deadly kind bandit!" He dropped to his knees and began frantically inscribing arcane symbols in the mud.

Meanwhile, the druid—his name couldn't possibly be Leafpuncher, could it?—screamed and bolted upright in his bush. Without opening his eyes, he grunted, laid back down, rolled over, and snored.

I tried to ignore the pain and get on my feet, but the attempt proved futile. Propped upright as well I could manage, I flipped notebook pages looking for Cause Minor Wound (I knew it was in there because it used the same components as Smell Magic, and this was my dried mistletoe notebook) but I had blood all over my hands and only succeeded in making a mess of the pages. Everything was happening so fast! The good news was that the bandits must have considered me incapacitated since no additional arrows followed the first. The bad news was that, by all accounts, they were right.

They were also ignoring Brukk, however, and the orc was anything but helpless. His summoning circle lit up in a flash of light and a burst of rancid smoke, which dissipated to reveal…

What appeared to be, as best as I could tell from my limited vantage point, another zombie squirrel. The poor thing let out a tortured squeak and limped away into the woods.

"For Ratlandia!" one of the bandits cried.

"For banditry!"

"For indiscriminate, random pillaging!" Since they were each about half the height of a human, it took two or three ratlings to carry each pack, and through the chaos I spotted a pair of them hauling my bag into the woods. My books were in there! My spell components!

The spirit orb.

Without that, our quest was over before it even began. I went for my mistletoe pouch, only to find that I still had a pinch of it—sticky with blood now, but usable nonetheless—between my thumb and forefinger. I flipped my notebook to the first page, and the very first spell I ever learned. Focusing my thoughts, I tossed the mistletoe to the wind and chanted the incantation to cast Magical Stamp on my bag.

The spell created an indelible, spiritual beacon that I could feel with something like a sixth sense. Alas, as the bandits fled into the forest, my magical link to the bag faded away with them. The effective range of the spell increased with practice, and I had only cast it six times in my entire life, today included.

"I take it back," Mae said, poking her head out from behind a tree. "*Now* we're well and truly fucked."

NOTES FROM HENK THE BARD:

Considering that the leather cover of *Rimbauld's Complete History of the Conquered Lands, Volume III* was quite soft, and the history contained within it was utter garbage, it actually made a better pillow than anything else. The book was one of Frinzil's most prized possessions, but I suppose there's no accounting for taste.

When someone's consciousness does become attached to their magical energy rather than their lifeless body, what you have is a ghost, but evidently NOBODY CARES ABOUT THEM.

The kobolds who built the Temple of Unrelenting Evil had ruled the Conquered Lands during the Nineteenth Age. By contrast, the tortoise mage-lich king war was far more ancient, marking the passage from the Second Age to the Third. Needless to say, The Conquered Lands didn't earn their reputation by being conquered, like, a *couple* of times.

Fun fact: Illusion smells *minty*.

It should be noted that, although the descendants of every civilization that had ruled the Conquered Lands considered it their ancestral home, ratlings were not one of those civilizations. As far as anybody knew, ratlings didn't even have an ancestral home—one popular theory was that they were created by magic sometime in the last century, possibly on a boat.

TURN UNDEAD

Adrenaline spent, I collapsed. Now that I had the opportunity to focus on it properly, the pain was all-encompassing.

"It's a good thing ratlings aren't one of the more deadly kinds of bandits," Mae said. "Because you people are absolute crap at fighting."

Brukk let loose a string of orcish profanities that would have made me blush if I'd had the capacity to feel anything other than blinding agony. Mae didn't know the language but certainly picked up the tone.

"The dark lord's gifts are not infinite," she said, shifting into her looming evil voice. "If you want me to waste my power on ratling bandits, I'll waste it. But I stood waiting for the command, and no command came."

I was more than cognizant of my utter failure as a leader—we had only survived the encounter at all because the bandits hadn't bothered to kill us. At the moment, however, there were more pressing concerns. "Medic!" I cried. "Somebody get the fiddlesticking medic!"

Brukk ran to the druid's bush, seized him by both legs, and

hauled him across the campsite toward me in a series of violent yanks. "Boss hurt!" he shouted over the druid's shocked waking-up noises. "BOSS HURT!"

"She used the word 'fiddlesticking' as a curse," Mae said. "How bad could it possibly be?"

Dumped unceremoniously at my side, the druid jerked his head around to look at Brukk, and then Mae. Finally, his gaze crossed the bloody, arrowy mess slightly below my right knee.

"Aaagh!" he said. "You should have somebody take a look at that."

I reached deep down inside and found the strength to feel exasperation in addition to the pain. "Yes, that is why I hired you," I said through clenched teeth.

His eyes grew wide, and he made a few more furtive glances around the campsite. I remembered that my own morning had started with similar confusion. As irked as I was, I didn't envy him the added complications of being literally dragged awake and immediately presented with surprise gore.

"Right!" he said. "Yes!" He placed one hand below the spot where the arrow protruded on my shin. "Uh, try not to flinch too much."

Then he wrenched the arrow out with one quick yank. Since the arrowhead was wedge-shaped, it tore more flesh on the way out than it had going in. Blood gushed from the gaping wound in spurts, and, for the record, I flinched *a lot*.

"There," the druid said. "Feel better?"

"WORSE! AAAAAAAAAAAAAGH! HOLY MOTHER OF PEARL, SO MUCH WORSE!"

Mae sounded genuinely perplexed. "Is this the first time you've actually *tried* to curse?"

"*Magical* healing!" I howled. "I need magical healing!"

The druid nodded. "Yeah, you do."

"From YOU. I need magical healing RIGHT NOW, FROM YOU."

"Oh! I'm, uh… pretty sure I don't know how to do that."

Brukk pushed the druid aside and began applying a wet mass of warm plant matter to the open wound (I hesitated even to wonder why it was warm.) He proceeded to wrap it tightly in a bandage made from his torn sleeve, and by the time he finished, the pain had diminished enough that I could at least focus on my surroundings.

"That should keep it in one piece," Brukk said. He glowered momentarily at the druid, who withered mournfully as directed. "It's a pretty small arrow, and it missed the bone, which seems good? If we find a potion or something before it heals on its own, I bet it won't even scar."

Brukk's left forearm, now bare to the elbow, was webbed with scar tissue and oddly bent as if a broken bone had never been properly set. His old party, it seemed, didn't have many healing potions to spare for a simple minion.

"Thank you, Brukk. Your expertise is greatly appreciated." It felt so much better I was even considering trying to stand. "What kind of vegetation dulls the pain like that?"

"Whatever kind!" he said proudly. "I just cram plants in there because that's what Wülf always did. The trick is to wrap it extra, extra tight until you can't feel anything."

Suddenly I was less confident in his medical acumen.

"Um, the Temple of Ustarros back in town has a free clinic…" the druid ventured sheepishly.

"Yeah, but the temples don't do any magic stuff either unless you can pay," Brukk said in orcish. "If it goes south and you wind up needing a pegleg, though, temple clinics are the best in the business. Fix you right up."

It was a grim thought—but then, our entire situation was grim. In addition to the orb, we had lost most of our supplies and all of our food. Ironically, the bandits had missed what was by far the most valuable thing any of us owned, since Brukk had managed to hide his teacher's spellbook in a thicket at the first sign of trouble.

Brukk had offered me the book as a gift—what if I accepted his offer, put an end to this entire fiasco, and used the book as tuition? It wasn't valuable enough to get me entirely caught up, but it might buy me enough time to figure something else out. The truth was, we'd had our first test as adventurers and failed it miserably. I had proved an utter disaster as a leader, and my party ranged from incompetent to openly hostile. I was also about ninety percent sure I could already feel the gangrene setting in on my leg. I had no business being out here. My place was back at the—

Sorcery Institute. It dawned on me that paying tuition had become the least of my worries. I had removed a relic from the Administrator's personal collection without permission and *lost* it. Never mind continuing my studies. If I returned without that orb, the Administrator could have me tossed in the city jail, or worse. My entire future had been stolen right out from under me, and now it was gone forever.

Unless I decided it wasn't.

What did I still have at my disposal? My map. Two of my notebooks and a limited supply of the spell components that went with them, which left me precisely eight tricks up my sleeve: Smell Magic, Magical Stamp, Cause Minor Wounds, Resist Itch, Overconfidence, Hypnotize Self, Duplicate Tome, and Transcribe. It wasn't much, but it wasn't nothing. And I had three fellow spellcasters who had, at the very least, signed up for this.

I rallied my troops. "The bandits took the orb, which we need if we're going to get the scroll before the others do." I was now more concerned about the orb than the treasure itself, but decided not to focus on that. "The ratlings caught us by surprise, but next time we'll be ready for them. Brukk, you're our pathfinder. Is there any chance you can track them?"

"Well, Wülf usually tracked stuff by looking for poop," he said. "That many… *ratlings*… would probably poop a lot. So, maybe?" There was no orcish word for 'ratlings,' so Brukk spoke just the one word in imperial common.

"Wait, did he say the bandits were ratlings?" the druid asked. "Were three of them identical sisters? Middle one seems shy at first but is actually the most sexually adventurous once you get to know her?"

Firstly, I had no idea how he thought I could possibly confirm that information. And secondly, ew. "There were three identical sisters, I think. I'm sorry, I know we were introduced last night, but I want to say your name is, um… Leafpuncher?"

"It's Sprig," he said. "But oh my gods, that's better." He gave me a solemn look. "Do you genuinely think I could pull off Leafpuncher?"

I had taken the druid to be a much older man, but by the light of day, it was mostly the thick, unkempt beard that gave that impression. Up close, he looked maybe six or eight years older than me, and reminded me a lot of a very particular type of university student—male, easygoing to a fault, and taking the Institute's lax policies on grooming as a personal challenge.

When pressed to stay on focus, Sprig was hesitant to share the specific details of his history with the bandits (which suited me fine) but insisted he could lead us to their hideout. It wasn't terribly close, but it was in the same general direction as the Temple of Unrelenting Evil, which was a stroke of luck.

"If anything, we might beat them there," he insisted. "Our legs are like twice as long as theirs, plus they'll probably stop along the way for more banditry."

Brukk helped me find a branch that would work as a walking stick, and I took a moment to cast a Resist Itch spell on my leg. It didn't do anything at all for the pain, mind you— Resist *Pain* was a category one spell, not a cantrip—but it was better than nothing.

For now, anyway. The entire theory behind sorcery was that most of the magical energy resided in the spellbook and the components, which reduced the physical toll on the spellcaster. Once a spell was cast, magic would slowly seep back into the page like a bucket collecting rainwater—for a simple cantrip like Resist Itch, the process would likely take a few hours, and I didn't expect the effect of the spell to last nearly as long. It was possible to cast a spell before its magic had replenished, but in that case, the energy came directly from the spellcaster's life force. Which didn't sound like a worthwhile trade-off for itch relief—I had once cast Ghostly Hand twice in succession when a key I was trying to retrieve fell back down a sewer grate, and the effort legitimately wiped me out for the rest of the day.

Casting dry also wasn't great for the parchment, and doing it too many times could burn out the spell, often setting the entire spellbook on fire. So that also wasn't great.

The sun was well past its peak by the time we got underway, and by late afternoon my entire body was sore from the stress of traveling injured. My leg itched so badly under Brukk's makeshift bandage job that I was calculating and re-calculating the length of time before my spell recharged. But then, there was also the issue of component management to consider—with my pack gone, I was limited to the mistletoe in my belt pouch, which wouldn't last forever.

Also, my stomach had finished settling and I was ravenous. I planned to take the main forest path southeast about halfway to the Temple of Unrelenting Evil, then cut due south into the wilderness to the spot Sprig insisted the bandits had their hideout. With my hindered mobility, we weren't even a third of the way to that halfway point.

"Perhaps we should stop for food," I said, remembering that we didn't actually have any food the moment I heard myself say it. Brukk's attempt at foraging earlier hadn't exactly inspired confidence. "Sprig, do you know if any of this nature is edible?"

"Oh, you can eat anything if you're hungry enough," he said. To demonstrate, he snatched something tall and green from just off the path, took a big bite out of the stem, and immediately spat it out. "Nope," he said. He tried again with some moss he found at the base of a tree and stared at me for a moment, chewing thoughtfully.

"Well?" I asked.

"I'm trying to decide if I'm hungry enough."

Through trial and error, Sprig eventually found some small, bulbous orange sprout things that were plentiful and almost flavorless, which was about the best I could hope for under the circumstances. Brukk made a fire to roast them over, which helped with the texture significantly.

Once the edge was off my hunger, I got to thinking. "Brukk,

tell me about summoning. Walk me through the process, step by step."

He was bent over the fire, working on the third batch of sprouts (he and Mae had also concluded that the sprouts were better than starving, while Sprig had eaten his fill raw and was resting peacefully against a tree trunk).

"There's not a whole lot to it," he said as he cooked. "First, I draw the circle with blood—like, the circle doesn't need to be all blood, but I need at least a little on my finger, for whatever reason. If I manage to draw everything exactly like the old man used to, poof, the squirrel shows up. Then I do the talking part that bends it to my will—I think I'm better at the first part than the second part." He thought about that for a moment. "I'm also not great at the first part."

"Can you summon anything bigger than a squirrel?"

"Hmm. I think I could do a wolverine." Then he took a sharp breath. "Wait, have you ever fought a wolverine? What if it comes out as a zombie? Have you ever fought a zombie wolverine?"

"You're the summoner," I said. "I don't think you're supposed to fight the wolverine." It seemed to me that confidence was a vital part of asserting control over a summoned creature, and the language barrier wasn't doing much for Brukk's.

"Have you tried doing the incantation in your native tongue?" I asked.

"How would the animals understand orcish, though?"

I let that hang for a few seconds. "Do you... think they understand *imperial common*?"

"I don't know, maybe? I guess I could try. With the squirrel, though, right? I don't know if I'm ready for—" he stopped, then jerked his head toward the wilderness. "Did you hear that?"

I hadn't heard anything.

"It's like a—" Brukk cocked his head. "There it was again!"

"What's he going on about?" Mae asked. "Remember, the rest of us don't understand the language of grunts and teeth gnashing."

"He hears something in the woods," I said, "and wants to know if we hear it too."

"I sure don't," Sprig said. "But that doesn't mean you don't hear it, brother. Only that our inferior human senses aren't up to the task."

Mae rolled her eyes. "Orcs don't even have supernatural hearing. *Elves* have supernatural hearing. And there's nothing out there."

"It could be the ratlings! Should I check it out? I'm going to go check it out." Before I could stop him, he disappeared off the path into the foliage. Considering that a moment ago he had sounded terrified at the prospect of fighting a wolverine, Brukk had certainly found his courage.

I didn't like the idea of splitting up the party, but he had left so quickly that I wasn't sure we could follow him if we wanted to. So we sat and waited, chewing on flavorless orange sprouts. After about fifteen minutes, just as I was getting worried enough to mount a rescue expedition, his head popped out of the bushes.

"I found something!" he said. "I think it's witch stuff."

He beckoned us to follow, and, not knowing how long we would have to wait for his return if we didn't, we stamped out the fire and pushed into the underbrush after him. After a short while, we came to a small clearing where massive slabs of black stone jutted toward the sky to form an imposing structure. The shape of a humanoid skull, quite realistic but at least twice the size it should be, was carved into one of the pillars.

"See?" Brukk said proudly, this time in common. "Witch stuff!"

Mae scrunched up her face. "What makes you think this has anything to do with witches?"

"Uh, scary bone shapes?" he said. Upon closer inspection, it wasn't only the oversized skull. The entire thing was covered in ominous-looking skeletal carvings.

"I think this is an altar to the undead," I said.

"That's not witch stuff," Sprig said in a frightened whisper. "It's vampire stuff!"

"That's actually a common mistake," I said. "The lich kings were the necromancers, and vampires were their undead generals. But they're both long gone, anyway. Necromancy was stamped out centuries ago."

"I don't know," Brukk said. "We used to fight zombies and stuff all the time. Somebody has to be making those things, right?"

"Well, the magic is famously long-lasting," I said. This was Third and Fourth age history, which was one of my specialties since it was covered in the only volume of *Rimbauld's Complete* that I actually owned. "Those zombies might be centuries old—it's not like they're getting any deader. Also, a lot of scholars think they buried hidden caches of undead soldiers in secret locations across the—"

I was interrupted by a low rumbling, coupled with a soft vibration of the ground beneath our feet.

"Okay, that I heard," I said when it finally stopped.

"Finally!" Brukk said. "It sounds like drumming, right? Only deeper and scarier, almost like a heartbeat, if a heartbeat was ancient and evil?"

Sprig jumped as a mound of loose earth was pushed up from the ground between his feet. Something with thin, spindly appendages began clawing its way out of the hole.

Brukk and Sprig screamed in unison.

"It's a lich king!" Sprig whispered after his scream petered out.

The creature was potato-shaped, with a dozen insect-like legs and a soft, pale carapace that looked as if it would explode with pus if you poked it. It was approximately the size of a rabbit.

"It's a zombie larva!" Brukk said.

"There's no such thing as a zombie larva," I said. From what I knew of necrozoology—which, admittedly, was not as strong as my necro*history*—this was a carrion crawler.

"Well, there was a whole swarm when we fought them, and based on how freaked out everyone was I'd say they're… medium-to-moderate deadly?"

So worse than ratling bandits. As leader, I didn't want to project weakness, but those bandits had very nearly killed us. And Brukk had been confident at the start of that battle. We instinctively drew close together for safety—even Mae—and it occurred to me that we should really have some kind of plan worked out in advance for situations like this.

The carrion crawler did not move.

"So is it undead, or just regular dead?" Mae asked after a moment's silence. "I feel like we could pretty much leave it here and head back to the path."

"No," I said. "We're taking this thing down." The crawler could be more dangerous than it looked, and I didn't feel right leaving it to terrorize the woods if that was the case. Besides, this was a perfect opportunity to get in some much-needed combat practice. "Mae, can you light it up?"

"Do you want me to? I mean, it's already dead. Is it going to be less of a problem or more of a problem if it's also on fire?"

Hmm. I knew a spell called Confuse Dead, but it was in one of my stolen books, and to be honest, the thing looked pretty confused already. "Brukk, would you care to try summoning something?"

"But what if I can't control it?" he said. "Then we have to fight a wolverine and a zombie larva. On fire."

"Do you even need to control it?" Sprig asked, maintaining his alarmed expression as if reserving the right to return to a state of whispering terror. "A lot of animals will just instinctively attack the undead on sight."

Brukk wasn't convinced. "So far most of my summons *are* the undead."

Sprig shook his arms and shoulders, psyching himself up. "Maybe I can, like, commune with something nearby. I mean, I'm a druid, right?"

"Are you, though?" Mae deadpanned.

He sat on the ground with his eyes closed, legs crossed, and both hands pressed down on the earth. "I think. Why else would I be wearing a druid robe?"

The school library had plenty of volumes on druidic magic, and I knew that Commune with Fauna was an established part of the tradition, so it was worth a shot. Meanwhile, the crawler had somehow managed to turn itself over onto its back, legs flailing helplessly in the air.

"Nope," Sprig said after a moment. "I think I can only commune with landscape. There's a whole network of werebadger tunnels in this part of the forest, though, if that helps."

"Ugh, you're all worthless," Mae said. She rolled her eyes, her pupils turning white mid-roll. The effect was quite unsettling. After muttering something under her breath for a few seconds, she gestured grandly toward the sky. "There!" she said. "A dire heron. Those things are the bane of all evil, and I should know."

Sure enough, a massive, long-necked bird was circling above us. Dire herons were significantly larger and more ferocious than garden-variety herons, and this one easily outweighed any two of us combined. They weren't intelligent enough to be classified as sentient but were certainly smart for birds, and were as anti-evil as you could hope to find in a woodland creature.

"This could work!" I said. The crawler had almost managed to right itself, so if we were in any sort of danger, it was increasing marginally. "How do we get its attention?"

"Hey!" Brukk shouted in common, waving his arms. "Bird! Fight death bug! So evil!"

The heron let out a majestic caw and pulled its wings tight against its body, plummeting toward the ground in a controlled fall. Just before impact, it pulled gracefully out of its dive, snatched the carrion slug up in its massive beak, and swallowed it whole.

"Holy Hragma hammer!" Brukk said as the heron flapped wildly and regained altitude without ever having touched the ground. He switched to orcish to better express is glee. "I can't believe it worked! That was the most amazing thing I've ever seen!"

I had to agree. And, more importantly, my party had come together to defeat an adversary using our collective intellect and combined experience. It was a much-needed boost of confidence and could only help bring us together as—

Before I finished the thought, the bird's massive, lifeless form fell from the sky and hit the ground with a wet thud a few feet from where we stood. It shuddered, then opened its eyes to reveal twin, lifeless voids where its eyeballs should have been. Throwing its head back, it let out a ghastly screech that echoed throughout the forest.

"Zombie dire heron!" Sprig whispered in terror.

This time the screaming was both in unison and unanimous.

NOTES FROM HENK THE BARD:

The bandits also left behind a few items strewn about that Mae hadn't bothered to put away after her rummaging, but the most valuable thing among them was a discarded ledger from a barrel-making business.

Five of Frinzil's eight available spells were in her mistletoe notebook (dried mistletoe was cheap, and the Institute imported it by the wagonload) and the other three required an iron nail, which fortunately wasn't consumed during casting. Technically she had access to Eyes of the Orc as well, because it was the only cantrip to require firefly paste and she had extra room in the iron nail notebook. But all her firefly paste was in her bag, so for now that one was also off the table.

In the third age, the lich kings had utilized vampires to lead their armies, but the mysterious, charismatic bloodsuckers had always gotten better press, so they remained in public memory long after their more powerful (and significantly more disgusting) masters were forgotten.

Commune with Landscape, for the record, was not an established part of the druidic tradition at all.

The entire concept of "evil" was nebulous, so even though a dire heron might attack an undead creature on sight, you couldn't necessarily rely on it to protest imperial corruption or help fight for safer mining practices, for example.

EXPEDITIOUS RETREAT

We scattered.

I ran as fast as my mangled leg would allow, which was, to be sure, not particularly fast. Brukk's bandages had worked wonders so far, but this was my first attempt at fleeing since taking that arrow to the shin, and my leg exploded in pain with the impact of the first stride. The others disappeared into the woods quickly, but there was no way I could keep up. I pushed forward through the pain as best I could, to the sound of branches snapping, feathers ruffling, and general undead shrieking behind me—the heron, mangled pretty badly from its fall, seemed to be having a very similar experience to my own.

And I am utterly certain that if it had been in even marginally better shape, I would not have survived to tell this tale. As I made it to the edge of the clearing, I risked a glance backward, only to see the big, dead bird barreling straight at me. Thus, when Sprig poked his head out of a hole in the ground, I just about tripped over it.

"Underground! Quick!" The hole was barely big enough to squeeze into, but I managed to drop down onto my belly, and

Sprig helped pull me into the soft dirt. The tunnel opened up into a slightly larger, dug-out hollow a few feet beneath the surface. Sprig helped me navigate further into the passage, both of us on our knees—his arms, for the record, felt much more sturdy than I would have guessed from the way his robe hung on his rail-thin frame.

"Werebadger tunnel," he said in a hushed tone. "Keep quiet—it might not know we're in here."

Sprig set me down about ten feet in, and I caught my breath as silently as possible. I made one gentle poke at my bandages before deciding I was better off leaving them alone until I was somewhere a little brighter and significantly less filled with loose soil. My eyes adjusted to the darkness just in time to see the heron's head appear in the hole I'd crawled through, where a tiny bit of sunlight filtered in.

Brukk's familiar scream came from somewhere behind me in the darkness. The heron screeched. "Well, *now* it knows, jerkwad," Mae said from elsewhere in the dark.

"Run!" Sprig yelled. There was a soft thud and a rain of dirt as his head collided with the tunnel ceiling. "Ow! No, crawl! But fast!"

I crawled as furiously as my injury allowed, and the heron's shrieks slowly faded behind us. "Why isn't it following?" I whispered after a few moments. "It's not that much bigger than we are. I think it could fit."

"It just died," Mae said. "Maybe it's not particularly eager for the cold, dark embrace of the grave?"

It was true that the first thing undead creatures generally did was to claw their way out of the ground, not down into it. Something bothered me about all of this, though—I mean, the almost-dying part, of course, but also on an academic level.

"That whole thing back there—zombies don't even work that way," I said. "You need a necromancer to raise the dead. It's not supposed to be communicable."

"You said there weren't any more necromancers," Brukk said, so quietly his voice barely registered.

This was all my fault. Because I thought the carrion crawler—a barely-moving potato bug—was too dangerous to leave be, we had unleashed a vastly more terrifying horror into the wild. And worse, now I was beginning to doubt everything I thought I knew about necromancy.

"Why are we still whispering?" Mae asked (still whispering, for the record). "And tell the orc to speak common."

"Tell orc self," Brukk whispered back. He understood the language considerably better than he spoke it. "Brukk not whisper from scary dead bird." He swallowed audibly in the darkness.

"Brukk whisper from *werebadgers*."

Wolves were the most common form of lycanthrope found in the Conquered Lands, but there were dozens of more obscure varieties. Granted, I didn't know much about any of them, but I had never even heard of werebadgers before today.

"Screw the werebadgers," Mae said. "If these tunnels connect to any of the deeper caverns, there could be goblins down here. Or troglodytes, or who even knows what else."

Our crawling was slow, but my mind was going a mile a minute. "We can only assume that the curse of the werebadger compels them to dig," I said. "If they continue tunneling, deeper and deeper, until they break through into existing caverns—"

I stopped as we came to the end of the tunnel, a thin shaft of light breaking through the darkness directly above us. "Okay, new theory. The werebadgers tunnel until daylight, at which point they turn back into people and basically just leave."

Sprig crawled beneath the hole and stuck his head and shoulders up into it, blocking out the light. The now-familiar shriek of the newly dead cried out from above.

"Crap!" he said, dropping to his knees. "How was that whole thing only thirty feet? Werebadger tunnels are the worst!"

"Crawl back! Crawl back!" I yelled. We scrambled several yards backward, and sure enough, saw the heron's head poke into the tunnel once again.

Sprig pressed both his hands against the soft dirt of the cavern wall. "There's another tunnel," he said. "It's real close, which is why I thought they were connected."

"And does it have any troglodytes in it?" Mae asked.

"I don't know, are troglodytes landscape?" he shot back. "Because if not THEN I HAVE NO IDEA." The stress was obviously getting to him, but there were more pressing matters at hand. The heron screeched again, and dirt clods fell through the shaft of light as it clawed at the tunnel opening.

"I can't help feeling this is all my fault," Sprig said. "I'll… I'll crawl back and distract it. You guys make a run for the other tunnel."

"We need you to even find the other tunnel, genius," Mae said.

"Brukk go. If Brukk summoner good, bird not scary-dead first place."

He was already scurrying back the way we had come. "Brukk, wait! I think it's losing its fear of cold, dark, grave embraces!"

"I'll flee!" he called back in orcish. "I can do this! I'm an excellent flee-er!"

As far as plans went, it was not a great one. Just as the heron looked like it had finally made up what was left of its mind to follow us into the tunnel, I heard Brukk screaming his head off from the other side. The bird yanked out its head, and I could feel its charge through the ground above us as the vibrations sprinkled us with a fresh layer of soil. Sprig leaped through the hole to the surface, pulling me up after him. The late afternoon sunlight was blinding after our stint in darkness, but there was no time to wait for our eyes to adjust. Fortunately, the next hole was just where Sprig said it would be.

As soon as we were back underground, Sprig and Mae began pushing forward into the darkness. "Wait!" I said. "Brukk! We can't leave him."

"So we should do what?" Mae asked. From the sound of her voice, she hadn't even slowed down. "Trade our lives for his? He was brave, okay? I admit it, the orc did something brave. But at this point he's either going to die or he isn't, and I'm not sure what we can—*ow!*"

A second cry of pain echoed hers in the darkness. "What you doing?" Brukk grunted. "Crawl other way! Bird on this side!"

The new tunnel was so short that Brukk had stumbled across its other end while fleeing. Which meant the heron was already waiting for us there.

Mae groaned. "So we're right back where we started."

"No," Sprig said. His face was pressed against the tunnel wall again. "We're thirty yards south of where we started. This whole region is riddled with tunnels. We can just do the same plan again. And again after that."

And so we did. This time, after drawing the bird's attention, Brukk crawled back to join us at the far end, and the heron didn't catch on until we were just about inside tunnel number three. Which was somewhat longer and also slick with mud for some reason, so that wasn't my favorite. Repeating the process again and again, we managed to travel mostly south (another benefit of communing with landscape was that Sprig could sense direction in his bones as if his entire body was one giant compass) for the rest of the afternoon. It was incredibly slow going, and after the sixth or seventh tunnel, Brukk returned to the opening and spotted the bird calmly waiting for him, having finally caught on to our trick. It had essentially outsmarted itself, though, because the four of us were all able to sneak into the next hole undetected, and for all we knew it waited there for hours.

I still wasn't about to risk open travel on the surface, but at least from that point on we were able to scramble in and out of the dirt in peace. After maybe the twentieth tunnel, night fell.

Some time later—hours, maybe? It was hard to judge time while crawling underground—we emerged from the final, southernmost badger hole collectively exhausted and entirely covered in a thick layer of grime. I wasn't sure exactly how long we'd been on the move, but it had been hours and hours.

"How do people do this?" I mused. "Adventuring, I mean. For days on end. Without bathing."

"Well, mostly it's not this much tunneling," Brukk said. "But, yeah, it gets pretty gross."

I was concerned about the effect copious amounts of dirt might have on my arrow wound, but then I remembered that my bandages were packed with random bits of foliage and who knows what else, and decided that particular ship had already sailed. At least the numbness had returned.

The moon was bright and high overhead—we hadn't seen

much of it in the thick of the forest during our stints between tunnels, but here the trees were much thinner. Reflected in the moonlight, I spotted a large stone structure across an open field.

Brukk's eyes followed mine. "Is it... the Temple of Unrelenting Evil?"

The building was about the size of a farmhouse but built like a castle keep, with attached stables. On closer examination, much of the open space between us and the structure was taken up by a big vegetable garden. Above it flew the imperial flag of Westerhelm.

My heart sank. "It's a watch outpost," I said. I saw a section of imperial highway just past the building, and the river beyond it, sparkling in the moonlight. "This is—" I paused, letting it sink all the way in. "This is half a mile from Dredgehaven."

Mae's tone was more open accusation than shocked disbelief. "You said we were going south."

"But... we should..." Sprig sputtered. "It was so dark, and the tunnels kept twisting around, like, root structures and..."

"You said you could sense direction in your bones as if your entire body was one giant compass."

"I can! It is!" Sprig furrowed his brow and made four points in the air in the shape of a diamond with his finger. "Wait, is south is the one that goes *up*?"

All that traveling. All that tunneling. I had borrowed a compass from the school the week before when I traveled around to triangulate the hunter spirit's target, but hadn't bothered to bring it with me to the tavern. Because I hadn't for a moment imagined the professional adventurers I'd hire *wouldn't have a compass*. Now I was so tired I was barely keeping myself upright, and I was right back where I started.

Further, actually, since we would have to pass through last night's campsite on our way to the forest path. Should we just sleep there again? Of course, assuming nobody at school had noticed the missing orb yet, I could just go sleep in my own bed. At least I'd get a bath in, and maybe something approximating medical attention. Then in the morning, I could…

Swing by the tavern to hire a different adventuring party? Hmm. The idea of breaking Brukk's heart by firing him was unthinkable. And Mae really wasn't the problem either. Sprig was the weakest link, for sure, but he was also the only one who could theoretically find the bandit camp, so I was stuck with him. Our chances of beating the veteran party to the temple were diminishing rapidly, but at this point, it was either push forward or just crawl into a hole and die.

I was carefully weighing my options.

We stood in silence for a moment as Sprig tried to make himself as small as possible. "To hell with it," Mae said at last. "I'm starving. I'm getting some vegetables."`

"What? Mae, you can't!"

She was already headed for the garden. "What, the denizens of evil aren't allowed to enjoy fresh produce?"

"No, you can't steal from the imperial watch!"

"Whatever, it's barely stealing," Mae said, not breaking her stride. "They don't even have rabbit fencing around it, it's a miracle there are any—"

She was interrupted by a screech that sounded as if it came both from the pits of hell and also just a short distance through the woods.

Brukk let out a yelp. "It found us! Back into the tunnels!"

"We'll be trapped!" I said. "From here they only go back toward the altar!"

"Which is the direction we're supposed to be going anyway!"

"Speak common, damn it!" Mae yelled.

A second screech came, louder and closer.

"To the outpost!" I screamed. "Run!"

Brukk threw one of my arms over his shoulder, and Sprig grabbed the other one. Together we scrambled into the vegetable garden and quickly caught up with Mae, who apparently hadn't decided if she liked her chances better with law enforcement or the bird monster. We dragged her along with us, and immediately, as if on cue, the ground gave way beneath our feet and dumped us straight into a pit. A circular iron grate twisted end-over-end above us and locked shut once we had passed through.

My fall was broken by something large and warm, covered in fur and approximately the size of a horse. It groaned and rolled over, dumping me onto the stone floor.

"Werebadgers!" Brukk said in a panicked whisper.

There were five of the massive beasts in there with us, taking up almost the entire space. We pressed against the curved, stone wall to give them as much room as possible.

"I think they're sleeping," Sprig said. "At least we're... safe from the heron?"

The badger I had landed on moaned again and shuddered. "Not for much longer, I think! Mae, please tell me you have something that will take out five groggy werebadgers."

"Are you fireproof? A Demonic Fireball would engulf this whole pit."

"We have to get the sentries," Sprig said, throwing his head back. "Help! We're in the pit! We're not werebadgers, but we're trapped with them in the werebadger pit!"

Several of the badgers made low, growling sounds, followed by the screech of the undead bird from somewhere above.

"Hey, asshole!" Mae whisper-yelled. "Way less screaming!"

"I can't alert sentries silently!" he whispered back.

"No," Brukk said softly, in orcish. "But I can."

He dug into a pouch on his belt and pulled out a stack of burlap squares, each about four inches wide with rough, frayed edges. Cycling through them quickly, he settled on one, studied it briefly in the moonlight, wiped some half-dried blood from a scrape on his arm, and dropped to his knees between two hairy, snoring mounds. His hands skittered across the floor, working with greater speed and confidence than they had on the tavern table or the campsite that morning.

With a flash and a puff of smoke, something small appeared before him. "By the seal of my blood," he said in orcish, "by the power of the ancient traditions, kneel before me, rodent. I bind you to my will!"

The squirrel chittered, then lowered its head in what might have been an attempt to bow, its healthy, lustrous fur reflected in a shaft of moonlight.

"I did it!" Brukk said. His breathing was heavy and his brow was drenched in sweat—unlike sorcerers, summoners drew every ounce the power they wielded from their personal reserves. "I can't believe I actually did it!"

Without warning, a wide column of blue light erupted from the stone floor, engulfing Brukk from below and lifting him about six inches off the ground. Then a second, narrower yellow column shone down on him from the night sky.

"What the fuuuuuuu…" Mae seemed to be the only one who wasn't quite shocked beyond words.

As he floated, suspended in the luminescence, distinct

markings appeared on the exposed flesh of Brukk's arms and face as if drawn with a brush, some as black as ink and others as white as polished bone.

"Summoning tattoos!" he said, still floating, tugging on his torn sleeve to find that the marks went all the way up his arm. Brukk was giddy with delight. "Just like the old man! This means I'm a real summoner!"

I could feel my jaw going involuntarily slack. I had seen markings like these before.

And that wasn't what they meant at all.

NOTES FROM HENK THE BARD:

As a general rule, the more descriptive words precede the name of a wild animal, the more dangerous it is. And if the first two words are *zombie* and *dire*, running is always a good policy, even if the third word is something as harmless-sounding as *heron*.

To be fair, you have to expect some gaps in your knowledge when most of your necrohistory comes from *Rimbauld's Complete History of the Conquered Lands*, because, again, garbage.

Despite being coined specifically in reference to werewolves, "lycanthrope" had become a catch-all term for all forms of cursed half-animal shapeshifters. The werewolves were still kind of pissed about it, actually.

The history of the Conquered Lands was an uninterrupted saga of conquest going back a thousand years. For all the vestiges of ancient civilizations that remained on the surface, however, others had been driven into the depths of the earth where they still thrived. Deep elves, goblins, troglodytes, giant, intelligent spiders—there was all sorts of stuff down there, and none of it was particularly hospitable toward intruders from the surface world.

BRUKK

The tribe of orcs Brukkthog was born into didn't have a name. They had been nomads for as many generations as anyone could remember—longer than Westerhelm had ruled over the Conquered Lands, at the very least. That particular empire welcomed orcs as soldiers and tolerated them as servants, but had little use for them under any other circumstance. When the tribe was occasionally blessed with fresh faces—having recently abandoned one of those two vocations, more often than not—the young Brukk would pester them relentlessly for tales of "civilization." In his imagination, this was a single, glimmering metropolis bursting with excitement and opportunity.

He got very little in return for his efforts, other than the occasional lecture about how orcs were better off keeping to their own kind. But if such reprimands were meant to stem his curiosity, they had quite the opposite effect.

Brukk was always particularly enraptured by legends of a great orcish city hidden somewhere in the wilderness, and every time the tribe packed up to wander further from encroaching civilization, his father insisted that they would finally discover it. They would, in due course, stumble across a hidden city of gnomes, a hidden city of elves, and a very well-secluded community of bugbears, but never the fabled city of orcs. By the time he was old enough to understand that it was nothing more than a comforting myth, Brukk knew that his father's life was not for him, and set out to find his place in the world of man.

His first real encounter with magic was when he was quite literally summoned by it. He had spent more than a month fruitlessly seeking work in Port Erraegard, the largest city in the Conquered Lands, when he was suddenly and inexplicably spirited out of the streets and into a foul-smelling cloud of smoke in a cold stone hallway.

A powerful summoner named Cromwallis needed assistance shifting rubble to free his companions from a collapsed section of ancient temple, and by random chance, Brukk was the minion his circle delivered to him. Brukk's will was no match for the summoner's, but the truth was, he would have helped even if he hadn't been under the old man's thrall. *Four people were trapped beneath a pile of rocks.*

The bond of mastery between the summoner and the summoned becomes more challenging to maintain over time, but Cromwallis found that control over his new lackey took very little concentration. In fact, performing menial tasks in exchange for food and some rudimentary form of lodging was the kind of work Brukk had been hoping to find anyway. The line between summoned thrall and hired hand slowly blurred, then dissipated entirely as Brukk settled into his new life as an adventurer's minion.

It was not an easy one. In all, he would spend nearly two years with the group, which once had to replace a dead party member twice in the same week (first the original priest and then his freshly-hired replacement, although the third priest was the kindest to Brukk of the three so he adjusted to the change fairly quickly). It occurred to Brukk that the party held some members in higher esteem than others—whenever the mighty half-orc warrior Krogos fell before their enemies, for example, they always found the gold to have him resurrected at a local temple. (To be fair, there happened to be enough of him left over to resurrect each time.)

Krogos never warmed up to Brukk. Even so, Brukk was enamored with the whole lot of them. The way the party took control of their collective destiny and literally carved their own path through the wilderness struck him as a noble and enviable way of life. Mostly, though, he was fascinated by the magic. No one had ever told him that orcs couldn't be magicians—growing up among the cast-outs, no one had ever told him that orcs could be anything except vagabonds and scavengers, subsisting on the edges of civilization while simultaneously trying to stay as far away from it as possible.

He saw the party's various priests create tiny miracles daily, but he also watched as they prayed to their gods for every spell, and offered up constant tributes to stay in the deities' good graces. Cromwallis the summoner, on the other hand, seemed to wield his magic entirely on his terms. Brukk had no way to know that much of that magic was bargained for, both from gods like those the priests worshiped and from much darker, more nefarious sources. Each one of the markings that covered the old man from head to toe was a debt, and the powerful beings that had granted him favor might come seeking payment at any time.

But Brukk could only see that the summoner commanded almost as much respect from his companions as he did from the creatures that appeared in his circles. He began studying his employer's rituals, at first from a safe distance and eventually from closer (and thus more dangerous) vantage points. He had never known exactly what he was looking for when he left the wilds, but his time with the adventuring party had convinced him that the practice of magic was his destiny. And one night, when the party had left him guarding their camp, he worked up the courage to attempt a summoning of his own.

The insectoid creature that materialized wasn't at all what he had intended to call forth. And it didn't even survive the experience, inexplicably falling dead and somehow catching fire just as soon as it appeared. Nevertheless, Brukk was elated. He vowed to continue his studies, and once he felt confident enough in his abilities, to go to Cromwallis and ask to be taken on as a proper apprentice.

Alas, he would never get the chance. An adventurer's life was dangerous and chaotic at best, and the slightest unforeseen complication could be the difference between life and death. Cromwallis fell to a tree kraken three short weeks later. Krakenfire only burns living matter, but consumes it completely, and Brukk was left to collect the old man's robes and other belongings from the heap of ash where they remained after the long, harrowing battle against the monster had been won.

Brukk's relationship with Cromwallis had been complicated, to say the least. But he knew that the party would need a new spellcaster, and during the long, lonely journey back to town, he decided he was the orc for the job.

It was high time Brukk began carving his own path as well.

NOTES FROM HENK THE BARD:

The Conquered Lands were crammed to the brim with hidden cities, truth be told, largely for tax-avoidance purposes.

While they left Brukk at camp, the party was using an elaborate combination of fish-breathing spells and weighted boots to loot a sunken temple at the bottom of a lake, which has nothing to do with Brukk's story but is still pretty neat.

Cromwallis, or "the old man," as his companions called him, was a gray and grizzled forty-nine years of age when he met his end. Although plenty of humans lived longer, you didn't run across many adventurers even approaching fifty who were still in the game.

CHAPTER SEVEN

CHARM PERSON

The runic markings that now covered every exposed inch of Brukk's flesh weren't some peculiar fashion statement popularized by summoners. Each one represented a debt owed to a particular god or demon, and the only way he could have acquired them—other than making a whole lot of pacts with a whole lot of cosmic beings on the sly immediately after falling into a badger pit—was by somehow inheriting them from his deceased mentor.

It made sense, I supposed, that debts to beings of such immense power would be passed along from master to apprentice—no god or demon would allow a matter as trivial as incineration to prevent them from getting their due. So in that sense, maybe Brukk was right—by whatever standards those gods and demons measured it, his success with the squirrel must have marked his official graduation into the ranks of practicing summoners.

For the record, his student debt made my own look like a pittance.

I'd have to set aside time in the future to ponder the ramifications of this, however, since the twin columns of light had also jarred awake five confused, hungry-looking werebadgers. The light faded, gently lowering Brukk to the stone floor.

"Fetch the sentries!" Brukk commanded his tiny minion. The squirrel scurried up the hard, stone wall to the rim of the pit—

Where it was promptly snapped up into the undead beak of the dire heron.

The bird shrieked again and shoved its head through the iron grate, stretching its neck as far as it could into the pit. We fell to the floor in an attempt to keep our heads attached to our bodies. The badgers, however, were less inclined to take this sudden invasion lying down. One of them leaped into the air, snapping its great jaws at the intruder.

"No!" I cried. Since everything I had ever learned about necromancy was evidently a lie, I was now terrified that any contact with the heron would only result in a zombie werebadger that we'd have to deal with. In all honesty, though, would that be any more dangerous than a normal werebadger?

Fortunately, we never had to find out. A wave of heat pushed down from above, and the undead bird withdrew its beak. Engulfed in flames, it emitted one final screech and fell silent somewhere out of view.

The effect of this spectacle on the werebadgers, however, was only to rile them further. But before any of them could take its frustrations out on us, a burst of darts, each about the length of my finger, rained down from above. All five badgers slumped into heaps of fur on the floor.

Sprig, who had scrambled to his feet in the apparent hope of reasoning with the beasts, slumped over on top of them.

"My friend is hit!" I yelled, rising to my own feet. With…

a sleeping dart? I hoped? "He needs medical attention!"

A figure appeared above us, his polished armor gleaming in the reflected light of the zombie fire. "The four of you aren't werebadgers?"

"No! We were chased into this pit by the—"

"Then you're under arrest," the watchman said. A second volley of darts followed the first. I felt multiple stings and heard exactly two more words before I hit the floor again and lost consciousness.

"For necromancy."

I awoke to the alarming sensation of liquid in my throat. Swallowing instinctively, I coughed hard and opened my eyes. I was in a plush leather chair, my hair and clothing uniformly damp as if I'd been caught in the rain and given an inadequate amount of time to drip dry. They must have doused us with water—it seemed to have washed most of the tunnel crud away at least. Judging by the vaguely medicinal taste, though, the stuff I'd swallowed wasn't water. Brukk and Mae were sitting to my left, in similar states of confusion and distress. To my right, Sprig lay on the floor in front of his chair, moaning.

"I think any more antidote might legitimately kill him— I've given him two entire vials already."

"He's... a sound sleeper," I said, repeatedly blinking until the speaker came into focus. He was an older man, Westerhelmian, and perhaps forty. He wore a sword at his belt but no armor, and a crest on his sleeve that probably marked him as a captain. Curiously, he also wore the symbol of

Takifuweli, the same goddess that Kuminik worshiped. I'd never heard of someone joining the Takifu Order who wasn't Tanneghede. But then again, the imperial watch was packed with Takifus—the fact that so many watchmen literally worshiped justice was what gave them their reputation for even-handedness—so it made sense that the religion would spread among the rank and file.

"I—I think there's been a huge misunderstanding," I said through one final, short coughing fit. "We're not necromancers."

"A novice sorcery student and a druid wildling? I would imagine not." The captain's eyes turned to Mae. "This one, however, has quite the ill-favored look about her. And *this*—" He gave the leg of Brukk's chair a slight kick. "I don't even know *what* I'm supposed to think about this. Have you clawed your way out from the pits of Hell, I wonder? Or are you just doing your level best to find your way into them?"

Brukk stared back at the captain in silence. His new tattoos made him look at least sixty times more intimidating than he had previously, and the effect was surprisingly chilling. We were in some sort of office or study—bladed weapons that looked more functional than ornamental lined one wall, and along another was a display case filled with maps, scrolls, and miscellaneous paraphernalia. None of my companions were restrained, and there was no one in the room but the four of us and the lone officer. Which meant that he either didn't think we were dangerous or was highly confident in his abilities. Either way, I was sure I could defuse the situation.

Mae, meanwhile, had finished her own coughing and sputtering. "Him?" she said, her voice dripping with disdain. "He's your worst nightmare. Or second worst, rather. Because when he's done with you, you'll still have me to deal with, and mine is the face that will haunt you on the slow, painful journey back to meet your maker. Do you understand me? *I am your doom.*"

I let out a low noise that was half sigh and half moan. "She's not your doom. She's not anybody's doom. She's just upset about getting shot full of darts in your badger pit."

"She should count her blessings. If she hadn't found the relative safety of our trap, she might have been incinerated alongside her undead abomination."

Now I understood what was happening. I couldn't fully explain the existence of the zombie dire heron myself. But if my first introduction to Mae had been alongside it, I might have also assumed that she was responsible, and wondered if necromancy had somehow returned to the Conquered Lands.

I wasn't sure how long we'd been unconscious—the room was lit by magic and windowless—but we had already wasted a day since the bandits had absconded with my orb. We needed to clear up this mess quickly and get back on their trail. Fortunately, if there was one thing that kept me in school so long—other than the staff being genuinely impressed by my unquenchable thirst for knowledge, presumably—it was my natural ability to suck up to authority figures.

"We have counted our blessings, sir, and consider the selfless devotion and impeccable judgment of the imperial watch chief among them." I went on to recount the day's travails, from the bandit ambush and the mysterious altar through the inconveniently short tunnels and into the werebadger trap. Every word of it was true—lying was the worst thing I could possibly do, since we weren't guilty of any crimes and also because I knew full well that I was a spectacularly bad liar.

Throughout my tale, the captain stared at me evenly, his face betraying no emotion. "Besides," I said in conclusion, "you know as well as I do that there are no necromancers in the Conquered Lands."

His lips stretched into a tight smile, but his eyes, if anything, hardened. "Of course there aren't. But there are no changelings, either, and that didn't stop us from burning out an entire village when one turned up unexpectedly in the elf warrens."

Mae leaped from her chair. "Bastard!" she shouted, throwing herself at the captain in an uncharacteristic fit of passion. A sphere of blue light flashed around the captain's hand, and with a casual wave, he sent Mae flying across the room into the display case, knocking various relics and scrolls to the floor.

Brukk followed Mae's lead, but before he even got to his feet, the captain raised another, similarly glowing hand, and Brukk dropped to the floor.

"I can only assume the witch was holding you prisoner," the captain said to me. "You may take your unconscious friend and go."

"No, we're not—"

He cut me off. "What I'm telling you," he said very deliberately, "is that you need not share her fate. Takifuweli demands justice of the necromancer and her devil orc, but—"

"Troubadours!" I blurted. "We're a band of traveling troubadours, researching a *play* about necromancy!"

I was in shock. Even though I had no idea what an elf warren was, the very idea that someone would use folk superstitions as a pretext for wholesale murder—and then gloat about it—filled me with rage. I had never heard such unabashed evil proclaimed so casually, as if the captain could hardly wait to confess it. All while wearing the crest of the Takifu Order.

The fact that it came from someone I had assumed was worthy of respect only made it worse.

"Troubadours," the captain said incredulously. "Researching a play. And yet you first felt the need to claim you were adventure seekers, because…?"

I had to think quickly. "It's a secret play."

"A secret play."

"Yes."

"About necromancy."

"A cautionary tale. Can you imagine what other troubadour—people?—would do if they heard what we were working on?"

"I'm certain that I cannot."

"Steal our idea, that's what," I said.

"Mm-hmm. And naturally, your primary concern was that I—a captain of the imperial watch currently interrogating you for the crime of necromancy—would steal the idea for this play."

"It's lightning in a bottle, sir."

Both of the captain's hands still glowed, and he held them out at chest height, fingers spread. Brukk was on his knees in front of his chair, and Mae was face-down at the base of the display case. They both made tiny grunting noises, but neither moved.

"That's a shame," the captain said, "as I have no need for troubadours at all. A group of powerful spellcasters, on the other hand—even those of a less savory variety—might prove themselves useful to the order."

I had no interest in being of use to the likes of him. "I don't think I got your name," I said.

"That is correct, you did not." He narrowed his eyes. "Do you know why so many Takifus make the long journey from

Tanneghede to safeguard a land that is not even their own?"

"Because they worship the goddess of justice, and their honor is beyond reproach." I can't imagine how my face looked when I said this because it felt like my whole body was sneering.

"Indeed it is," he said. "But they could certainly practice law enforcement in their own country rather than traveling halfway across the globe. The reason they come to these shores is that our lady Takifuweli, praise be to her name, is not a Tanneghedian goddess. They found her here, centuries ago, when Tanneghedes were the first of all humankind to set foot in this land."

His eyes shone as if reflecting some unseen fire. "She helped the Tanneghedes wrest control of the continent from the centaurs who had befouled her country, and she will smile down on her dedicated servants again when we rise up to beat the western usurpers back into the sea."

He was making a play for dominion over the Conquered Lands. Of course he was—everyone was *always* making a play for dominion over the Conquered Lands. Never mind that he himself was one of those western usurpers, or that the history of the conquered lands was essentially usurpers all the way down. It was obvious that this man's lust for power had little to do with anything the Takifu Order stood for. It was remarkable how those in power always managed to define "justice" as whatever would keep their boot on people's necks.

"Now," the captain continued, "your friends can enjoy the hospitality of our holding cell while they await the arrival of a prison transport. Or you convince me that our hallowed lady Takifuweli can make use of any special skills they might have beyond a proclivity for song and dance."

NOTES FROM HENK THE BARD:

Changelings were fairy tale boogeymen invented to frighten children. Why anyone would need to frighten children with imaginary creatures in a land filled with troglodytes, multiple species of kraken, and *scorpion bats* remains a mystery.

Tanneghede was actually the second human civilization to rule the conquered lands, not the first—the Omaki were there fully two centuries earlier. Or possibly third, depending on how you count, since the lich kings were technically human when they arrived.

Tanneghede society generally rejected god-worship along with most forms of magic entirely, and as a result, was the most scientifically advanced civilization outside of the gnomish enclaves. In their homeland, the Takifu order was viewed as something of a religious cult, which was certainly one of the reasons so many of its members went abroad.

The captain's coup wasn't fated to succeed, of course. This book wasn't even written until after the dawn of the twenty-third age, which certainly didn't mark the ascendancy of renegade Takifus led by a corrupt white guy.

BEACON OF HOPE

The rough, bare stone wasn't at all comfortable, but at least the place was lit—if poorly—by a row of torches just on the other side of the rusting iron bars. The smoke from those torches was enough to make my throat itch, although some of that could be attributed to animal stench, since the holding cells and stables were apparently in the same building.

"That was a revelation," Mae said, a smidge of genuine respect lighting up her usually impenetrable expression. "Personally, I would have gone with the whole claiming-to-be-necromancers angle, then tried to escape later from Takifu necromancer training camp or whatever. But what you did back there took nerve."

The thing was, I *had* tried to convince the captain they were necromancers. I had just done it very, very poorly.

"I mean, open, contemptuous mocking? To the point where he went ahead and threw you and the druid in here with us? Huzzah. Seriously, respect is due."

Sprig had managed to remain asleep throughout the entire incident, including being dragged feet-first down a stairwell, and was presently snoring away in one corner of the cell.

Brukk was far more somber than Mae. "I'll never forget this," he said in orcish. "You could have abandoned us to our fate, but you threw away your own freedom to keep the party together." His chin began to tremble. "I just—you don't know what—"

"Oh, piss off," Mae said, seemingly mistaking his earnest gratitude for a rebuttal of some kind. "That shit was prodigious, and you know it." She was more cheerful and upbeat than I had ever seen her. By a considerable margin.

"You don't seem worried by our predicament," I said.

Mae grinned, which was moderately horrifying. "That's because, unlike some people, I had a plan back there." She drew a roll of linen parchment sealed with a blob of gold wax from beneath her cloak. It was one of the relics from the display case in the captain's office.

"Like I give a single, onerous crap what happens in the elf warrens," Mae said. "Now, use this to blow a hole through that wall or whatever, and let's get out of this cesspool."

I gently peeled open the wax and unrolled the parchment. "This is a priest scroll."

"Right. Isn't that what you are?"

"What? No, I'm a sorcerer. A priest gets their power from—" I stopped myself. The lesson in comparative magic studies could wait. "Only a priest can cast this. Specifically, a priest who worships Takifuweli." I examined it more closely. "Also, I think this is a healing spell."

"*Uuuuuuugh*," Mae said, the familiar exasperation returning to her face. "Well, at least you can finally fix your stupid leg."

"Yes, if I were *a priest who worships Takifuweli*. Are you not paying attention to any of this?"

Before the argument could escalate, we were interrupted by the sound of an iron gate opening nearby. The golden pink light of dawn flooded the cell, which either meant we had spent longer unconscious than I'd guessed, or that time spent bickering in jail went by surprisingly fast.

"Nine prisoners for transport," a tired voice said from around the corner. It momentarily reminded me of life growing up in the manor—"transport at dawn" was exactly the sort of thing lords and ladies were always demanding without even considering that people who actually worked for a living would have to—

Wait a minute. Did I recognize that voice? The moment he stepped into view, my heart leapt with joy.

"Kuminik! You have no idea how happy I am to see you!"

"Ugh," Mae muttered. You know this guy?"

The surprise on Kuminik's face melted into sorrow. "Oh, Frinzil. I know getting kicked out of school must have been a blow, but *necromancy*?"

"What? No, we're not..." I noticed him wince as he appraised my companions. "There are no necromancers," I said, "that's not even a—"

Kuminik cut me off. "To fall in with such an unsavory crowd..." Now he looked honestly befuddled. "Frinzil, it's been a day and a half."

"I didn't fall in with them, I hired them. I'm just trying to earn the money to—"

He shook his head mournfully. "It's not too late to turn yourself around. It won't be easy, but just keep your head down, serve your sentence..."

He glanced at the written order he was holding, and something stopped him in his tracks. When his eyes again met mine, he looked utterly heartbroken. Four guards with spears came around the corner behind him.

"Kuminik, listen," I said, as plainly and steadily as I could. "The captain of the guard is no Takifu. He's recruiting an army of spellcasters to stage a coup…"

"You take care of yourself, Frinzil," Kuminik said, and now it sounded like he was holding back tears. He took a sharp breath as if he was going to say something else, then scrunched up his face and turned to walk away.

"Wait!" I shouted after him. "I know it sounds like… just let me explain…"

He was gone.

The guards who replaced him wore plain leather armor with skirted leggings designed to let their long, rough tails whip freely behind them, and leather caps on their scaled heads. They were lizardfolk, and their uniforms were not those of the imperial watch. Two of them ushered Brukk, Mae, and me toward the gate while the other two dragged Sprig behind us.

Mae shot me a glance that said she still blamed me for not being able to break through a stone wall with a priest's healing spell. It barely registered, though—I was still reeling from the look on Kuminik's face when he read his order. We stepped out into the morning light, where several horse-drawn carts were waiting for us.

Brukk looked like he was on the brink of full-blown panic. "Brukk know lizardmen!" he said to our captors. "Lizardmen good people! Lizardmen not—"

"Lizardmen?" one of the guards said. "What is it with all you people and your gender assumptions? Lizardfolk males rarely even do manual labor. I'd wager that every single 'lizardman' you've ever met was a woman."

I groaned. The term 'lizardmen' had long since fallen out of favor for the more inclusive 'lizardfolk.' "He doesn't mean to offend!" I said. "His imperial common isn't the best, and—"

The guard spat on the road. "The witch and the orc go into high-security," she said to the others. "Throw these two into the crate with the badgers."

Fortunately, that last bit sounded considerably worse than it turned out to be. The crate was simply a large, general-purpose transport container, and the werebadgers had transformed back into human men at daybreak. Three of them were Muddledfolk like me, one was Westerhelmian, and the fifth appeared to be Omaki. All five looked utterly desolate.

"Tell me it didn't happen again," one of them muttered, more to himself than to his companions. "Tell me I didn't do anything…"

"Relax, brother," another said. "They lured us into that pit with vegetables, I'm sure of it."

"Oh, thank the gods," the first man said, gently sobbing into his hands. "I can't face waking up one more time covered in chicken feathers."

The group continued in their shared commiseration, but I had resigned myself to sulking alone because I was pretty sure I'd figured out why Kuminik was so distraught to learn our fate. We were trotted about fifteen minutes down the bumpy highway and then sat waiting for maybe a half-hour before our crate was loaded by crane onto a barge.

Which confirmed my suspicions. The imperial highway ended in Dredgehaven, which meant the best way to reach any of the river towns beyond it was by boat. The largest of these towns, about twenty miles downriver, was a lizardfolk settlement. It had an actual name, but most people simply called it "the Arena" because that was the only reason anybody ever visited.

We were being hauled off to fight.

Ironically, as we floated south, we made much better progress toward the bandit camp than we had at any point during the previous day. The watch hadn't bothered to take my belongings, so I took out my map and unfolded it. If we somehow managed to jump ship halfway to our destination, we could cut east through the forest and—

Who was I kidding? As a professional adventurer, I was an abject failure. In the space of thirty-six hours, I had managed to have my quest hijacked, my magic orb purloined, had been chased by an undead heron into a pit, and sentenced to fight in a gladiatorial arena. By now, the veteran party was surely nearing the Temple of Unrelenting Evil. And the orb—the priceless relic without which my academic future was decimated—could be anywhere.

None of which, in all honesty, even mattered, Because even if I had been a proper graduate of the Sorcery Institute—even if I had mastered the single field spell that would earn me a certificate rather than my endless list of useless cantrips, and even if most of those cantrips hadn't disappeared along with the orb—I still couldn't hope to survive two minutes as a gladiator. I was an abject failure who was being carted off to inescapable death.

There were two short moans and a muffled yelp beside me, and Sprig bolted upright from his spot on the crate's floor.

"Did I do it?" He stared at the group of recovered badgers with glassy eyes. "Did I turn them back into humans using empathy and the lost art of—wait, are we moving?"

I couldn't muster a response.

"I'm sorry," Sprig said. The shifting light filtering through wooden slats above us accentuated his forlorn expression. "It's just—when I first wake up, I can't tell which part's real and which part's the dream, and I get all confused."

He dropped his head into his hands. "But the dreams are always different, and the days are always the same." He stared at the former badgers and the clear blue sky through the slats. "Okay, this part isn't exactly the same. What's actually happening right now?"

I sighed. "You did do it," I lied. I didn't even look at him to see if he was buying it, but I can't imagine that he was. "You saved us all from the werebadgers, but then I screwed everything up, and we're being sent to fight in a gladiatorial arena. It's hopeless. I'm sorry. The quest is dead."

"Man," Sprig said somberly. "Rough. That was the old quest, though. What about the new quest?"

I squinted at him. "What's the new quest?"

"I don't know, what was the old quest?"

"*Uuuuuuuuuuugh.*"

"No, I'm being serious. Tell me what the quest was. I want to help."

I had already spent more than enough time dwelling on my failure and was hardly in the mood to hash out the particulars with Sprig—or with the five morose werebadgers, who were now listening politely. Then again, it wasn't like I had anywhere else to be.

"Our quest was to retrieve the ancient, priceless scroll from beneath the Temple of Unrelenting Evil before a party of much more qualified adventurers found it first."

"Right, right," Sprig said. "No, I remember that part. But why?"

"Because it's—" I might as well be completely honest. "Because I don't even want to be an adventurer. I just want to go back to school and study magic forever, and the scroll was valuable enough to get me caught up on tuition."

"Aha," Sprig said. "So, is there any other way to go back to school? Other than finding an expensive old scroll?"

I briefly considered this, but my heart immediately sank again. "There would have been, maybe. But I borrowed... I stole the Administrator's spirit orb and lost it. Without that, I can never go back. And who knows where those bandits are, or what they've done with it by now."

Sprig's eyes lit up. "I do! I told you, I've been to their hideout! They hoard treasure like crazy. They have precious junk piled up all over that place."

This gave me pause. "You don't think they'll just sell it or whatever?"

"Something that weird and sparkly? I know they won't. So I ask you again: what about the new quest?"

I experimented with the sliver of hope, trying it on to see how it fit. "The new quest is to steal the orb back from the bandit hideout and return it to school."

"That's part one of the new quest, sure," Sprig insisted. "Part two is to earn money for tuition some other way. You can even keep my share—I don't actually care about the money. I just want..."

He gave me a look that broke my heart a little. "I want a reason to look forward to the days as much as I look forward to the dreams."

There was a hush throughout the crate, and one of the werebadgers sniffed and wiped a tear. Which reminded me of their presence and, in turn, of our shared predicament.

"Part one might actually be figuring out how to escape from a gladiatorial arena," I said.

"Well, how do people usually escape from gladiatorial arenas?" Sprig asked. "To be clear, this isn't that thing where I already know the answer and I'm trying to get you to say it out loud. I'm genuinely asking."

After a moment, a werebadger raised his hand.

"Um, yes?" I had taught Professor Grimgaffler's introductory classes plenty of times in his absence and slipped very naturally into the role. I pointed at the werebadger. "You, in the shredded tunic."

"Full-scale gladiator uprising?" he offered hesitantly.

"Hmm," I said. "Full-scale gladiator uprising." I didn't hate the idea. "Okay, walk me through it."

I hoped Sprig was right about the bandits hoarding treasure indefinitely because, to be honest, full-scale gladiator uprising was a bit of a long game. Nevertheless, it was the only plan any of us could come up with. And the more time I spent with the werebadger group, the more I was resolved to include them, along with as many other gladiators as possible (the badgers had yet to meet Brukk or Mae but already seemed quite invested in their well-being).

At any rate, the seven of us had plenty of time to brainstorm since our journey took the better part of the day. This included two full hours docked on the side of the river to investigate a persistent leak somewhere on the barge. At which point a bucket of water and several loaves of only moderately stale bread were lowered into our crate, so at least we were fed.

I managed to get a few hours of fitful sleep on the cold, increasingly damp wooden floor after we started moving again—unlike Sprig, the only rest I'd had in twenty-four hours had been while tranquilized at the outpost. My leg pain, for what it was worth, had lessened considerably—this was, after all, the longest stretch I'd had since the injury without any hiking, fleeing, or tunneling. As the pain diminished, the itch only grew, but plenty of time had passed since my last Resist Itch spell, so I cast it again before settling down.

I was awoken by the shouts of dockworkers and a heavy, wooden scrape that I could feel through the floor, immediately followed by an unsettling sensation of weightlessness. We were, I realized once I'd managed to get my bearings, being unloaded from the barge. We continued (by carriage, based on the bumpiness) for just a few minutes before coming to a stop. While we sat and waited for whatever was going to come next, Sprig and the werebadgers were eager to fill me in on the rough details of what they felt was a fairly solid blueprint for a full-scale gladiator uprising:

Stage I: Reunite with Brukk and Mae in captivity and make sure they were all right.

Stage II: Earn the trust and respect of fellow gladiators through a combination of ethical behavior, small displays of whatever limited kindness was possible in gladiator jail, and a strict policy of mercy in the gladiatorial arena.

Stage IIb: Do not get killed in the gladiatorial arena.

Stage III: Either A) convince the crowd-favorite alpha gladiator to join our cause or B) defeat the crowd-favorite alpha gladiator in combat, thus becoming the new crowd-favorite alpha gladiator, but refuse to deliver the killing blow to the previous one, resulting in the aforementioned (albeit begrudging) trust and respect.

Stage IV: Systematically win the crowd to our side, inspiring within the spectators a solemn reevaluation of gladiatorial combat as sport (and, ideally, of themselves).

Stage V: Possibly bribe a guard? Maybe? The option of seduction, according to Sprig, at least, was also on the table.

Stage VI: Something, something, escape.

The later stages were not nearly as well developed as the earlier ones, and I thought IIb, in particular, would require a great deal more fleshing out. Such concerns would have to wait, though, because the top of our crate opened with a crash and a rope ladder came tumbling down from it.

"Out, all of you." A guard armed with a crossbow peered through the open hatch and gestured at us to climb. "Welcome to the coliseum."

The coliseum, it turned out, was enormous. The land it was built upon was carved out of the forest, and from the thick growth crowding around the furthest boundary of the edifice, it appeared that Gluumwilde wanted it back. The arena itself, and the tourism-related businesses that had sprung up around it, were the biggest industry throughout the river towns south of Dredgehaven. As we climbed out of the carriage, a massive roar erupted from inside the open-aired structure. Judging from the sheer volume, there must have been thousands of spectators inside.

They did not sound as though solemn reevaluation of anything was foremost on their minds.

The guard motioned toward a fenced holding pen with her crossbow. "Make one wrong move—even think about moving wrong—and you get a crossbow bolt. Understand?"

"What's his problem?" Sprig muttered under his breath.

"*Her* problem!" I muttered back. "The men have fins on their heads." The guards were wearing smooth skullcaps, which struck me as unnecessarily gendered. But there was no time for discussing the finer points of lizardfolk gender politics. "It's just, they seem sensitive about it, okay? So don't make things worse."

The holding pen contained a wide assortment of humans and non-humans alike, but Brukk and Mae were not among them. A lizardperson in chainmail armor with a crossbow at her side kept trying to address the group but was repeatedly interrupted by crowd noise. I made a quick headcount, which left me with a sinking feeling in my stomach. Including myself, Sprig, and the werebadgers, there were twenty-two prisoners in the pen, plus however many might be in high-security with Brukk and Mae. Did the coliseum get this many new arrivals daily? If so, gladiator turnover had to be—

I pushed the thought to the back of my mind. The match inside had finally come to an end, and our guard launched into what amounted to gladiator orientation. It was essentially a list of potential offenses, most of which were punishable by death in the form of an unarmed match at the earliest opportunity against whichever horrendous beast had gone longest without food.

"Disobeying a direct order," the guard said, "death by combat. Disrespecting a guard or other member of the coliseum staff: death by combat. Fighting with other gladiators outside the arena: one day without meals. Any physical contact with a guard or other member of the coliseum staff: death by—"

A roar went up from inside the arena, and the guard rolled her eyes so hard they almost popped out of her head. Then a loud, echoing voice cut through the din.

"LADIES AND GENTLEMEN, YOUR NEXT MATCH!" It was the coliseum announcer, using some bit of sorcery or engineering to amplify their voice that I had never encountered before. "AT THE WEST GATE, STRAIGHT FROM THE DEEPEST PITS OF THE FORSAKEN REALM…"

(Slight pause for dramatic effect.)

"THE NECROMANCER WITCH AND HER TAT-TOOED DEMON ORC!"

NOTES FROM HENK THE BARD:

Lizardfolk had ruled the Conquered Lands during the Fourteenth Age, and although there was a common misconception that they were related to tortoise mages, the two were completely different species. Lizardfolk didn't have protective shells, for starters, or deep connections with an ancient, primordial evil that should never have intersected with the fabric of our reality. So those were two important differences right there.

Although Westerhelm had originally wrested control of the continent through military might, their enduring strength was the efficiency of their bureaucracy. As long as communities within their borders agreed to obey imperial laws and pay imperial taxes, they were left mostly to their own devices, up to and including gladiatorial combat for entertainment purposes.

The worst any of the werebadgers had to atone for appeared to be the wholesale mistreatment of livestock, so there was a silver lining, at least.

Also, a group of werebadgers is called an *excavation*, which is kind of fun.

The mighty river that passed through Dredgehaven branched out into several tributaries known as the "Fingers" as it flowed south—the arena was situated at the fork the Fourth Finger and the Thumb (which isn't how hands work, but you know, I'm not the one who named them). Don't even get me started on the Sixth and Seventh Fingers, which were only charted after they had already named the other five.

CHAOTIC GOOD

Oh, no. The high-security crate must have been loaded onto a separate barge, which going when ours had stopped for repairs, delivering Brukk and Mae to the arena much sooner. And now they were already up for their first fight, thanks to...

"AND AT THE EAST GATE! FROM DARKEST GLUUMWILDE, UNDEFEATED IN TWELVE STRAIGHT MATCHES! THE MAMMOTH, MULTIHEADED MAULER ITSELF, THE *MEGA-BEEEEEEEEAAAAAAAR!*"

Insubordination? Disrespect? General sass? If the guards were at all strict about the death by combat policy, Mae would have had enough time to sentence herself several times over before finishing orientation. A megabear was a savage monstrosity that looked like a grizzly with three heads, each of which at least twice the size of a standard bear head, since the entire creature was at least six times the size of a standard bear. With the possible exception of the long-extinct dragons and certain species of kraken, megabears were probably the most feared creature ever to roam the Conquered Lands.

Our timetable for full-scale gladiator uprising was going

to have to be curtailed considerably.

"Fellow prisoners!" I proclaimed as the crowd noise abated. "If we band together the guards won't be able to—" Something happened in the arena, and my words were drowned out by cheering. I realized that if there was any hope of saving Brukk and Mae, I was going to have to lead my ad hoc gladiator uprising *into* deadly combat rather than away from it, which would be an even tougher sell.

"Wait!" one of the werebadgers said. "We didn't gain their trust and respect yet! You're skipping ahead!"

"The necromancer and tattooed orc are Mae and Brukk!" Sprig said, the panic in his voice palpable. "That's stage one! They're fighting right now!"

"Wait. Your friend is a necromancer?"

The guard cocked an eye ridge but didn't bother adjusting her tone. "Attempting to foment a gladiator uprising," she said. "Death by combat."

"Don't listen to her!" I said. "We outnumber her twenty to one!"

"*Her*?" the guard scoffed. "Oh, because only *female* lizardmen can be arena guards? That's it! Death by combat!"

It dawned on me that if one was issued a helmet not designed for them, one might flatten their fin against the side of their head and wear it anyway. I was slightly mortified that I'd misgendered our captor, but there was no time to worry about that now. A chant broke out from the arena, not quite in unison, making it difficult to make out the words. It grew louder and louder, though, and sounded something like "ill-dah-ish, ill-dah-ish."

Then I caught it. *"Kill the witch."*

"He just wants to set us against each other!" I said, only

partially successful in my attempt to be heard above the chanting. "Keeping us divided is the only power he has!"

"I don't know," one of the werebadgers said. What had presented as a united front back in the relative safety of the transport crate was unraveling quickly. "The crossbow also seems like it could be considered a power?"

A thunderous crash cut through the din, and the entire arena wall shook, showering us with bits of rock and dust. The crowd noise rose to new heights, but there was now an edge of panic as if some portion of the cheers had been replaced with screams.

Another lizardperson appeared from inside the open gate, out of breath. "Get the prisoners into general population! Now! We'll sort them later!"

The two guards began hurrying us through the gate. Sprig and I were the last in line, however, and the orientation guard raised his crossbow and blocked our path.

"You two rabble-rousers can cool off in the pen," he said, kicking a lever with his foot that dropped the door between us. His muffled yell came from the other side of the closed gate. "And think about what you've done!"

From the noise, it sounded like the crowd's panic had escalated to full hysteria, and Sprig looked like he was ready to join them. "What do we do? Run? I could maybe boost you over the fence!"

"No." I was a hundred percent certain it was a terrible idea, but I didn't have another one. "Our friends are in there, and we're going in after them."

"Right!" He blinked. "How?"

It was a good question. Okay, time for a quick inventory: I still had Mae's scroll, but even if I could cast it, it was no use here. I also had my two spell notebooks, which left me precious few spells: Resist Itch, Smell Magic…

Suddenly, I had a plan. And again, it was not great. "You're going to do it," I said. "Druids draw their power from nature, and look!" I gestured to the nearby forest. "Nature!"

"But I don't even know if I am a druid!"

"Of course you're a druid—why else would you be wearing druid robes? Yesterday you communed with the earth itself, sensed the hollows within it, and saved us all. I know you can do this."

In truth, as far as I knew, there was no druid spell called Commune with Landscape, but Sprig had managed to navigate those tunnels somehow. He might not be a druid, but he was definitely *something*, and I was hoping he had another trick up his sleeve. If he was going to pull it out, though, the first step was believing that he could. Fortunately, I didn't have to rely on my skills as a motivational speaker on that front. I rifled through my notebook with one hand and grabbed a handful of dried mistletoe from my pouch. This spell required more than just a pinch, and would deplete almost half of my remaining supply.

"*Anarengu gareech nnnaruelia semmneng.*" I felt the energy flowing through my arm and into my fist, where I'd balled up the mistletoe. My palm tingled as the mistletoe was consumed, and I hurled the resulting ball of magic at Sprig like an invisible stone. The spell was called Overconfidence, and it was generally used to coax opponents into making some foolish mistake. I was hoping, however, that in this instance it would draw something out of Sprig that he had forgotten was even there.

"You're the most powerful druid in all the Conquered Lands," I insisted. I was still a dreadful liar, but Sprig was too spell-drunk to notice.

Sprig gasped, then shot me a mischievous grin. "Oh, you want to see some druid magic?" He strode up to the gate and laid both his hands on it. For a moment, nothing happened.

Although I'd studied them in theory, I had never seen the druidic arts practiced with my own eyes. So I didn't know exactly what to expect, but if any magical energy was coursing through the ground from the ancient trees of Gluumwilde to collect within Sprig's utterly still form, it was certainly taking its time. Hmm. Was it possible that he had merely found that robe somewhere in the woods? Or stolen it from a real druid who he had stumbled across unconscious?

Just as I was about to give it up as a lost cause, the wooden gate exploded with life. Pulsing branches pushed their way out and upward, bursting with newly sprouting leaves over the stonework of the arena wall. Living bark formed over the wooden planks, tightening around the gate's iron reinforcements. Roots forced their way into the trampled, hardened dirt. As Sprig stepped back to admire his work, tiny white flowers bloomed high in the branches against the backdrop of gray stone.

Sprout Timber was *absolutely* a druid spell, and judging by the enthusiasm with which life had burst from the long-dead wood of the arena gate, Sprig was no novice druid. He placed a hand in the mass of living foliage and shook.

It didn't budge even a fraction of an inch.

The look of triumph drained from his face. "I think I actually made it sturdier. Wait, why did I think I could do this again?"

Overconfidence was not a particularly long-lasting spell. Still, we were on to something! If Sprig could make wood beams come to life that dramatically, there was no telling what else he could—

Suddenly, the beams in question burst open in an explosion of splinters and sap, knocking Sprig off his feet and into the corner of the pen. Which was fortunate, since a less angled trajectory would have put him directly in the path of the two-ton, three-headed monstrosity that came charging through the mangled gate and plowed right through the fence beyond it.

Mae and Brukk followed behind the megabear, causing significantly less damage on their way.

"Brukk! Mae! You're—"

"Wait!" Brukk said in orcish. "Our stuff—I saw where they were keeping it! Be right back!" He bolted back into the arena, past a stampede of wide-eyed gladiators sprinting toward freedom and a platoon of coliseum guards behind them who looked far more concerned with the rampaging megabear than any escapees.

"What stuff?" I called after Brukk. "The bandits stole all our—" It was too late. He was gone. What was happening?

I turned my attention to Mae. "What is happening?"

"They're going to kill him!" Mae said. "We have to do something!" Her cloak was torn and her face was streaked with tears—seeing Mae so distraught was almost as big a surprise as the whole gate/bear explosion. Her attention was focused entirely on the beast, which was quickly encircled by guards with crossbows. They began firing bolts into its thick hide.

"How did you do this?" I gasped. "Are you controlling it?"

"No! I—I just made friends with him, okay?" A river of spectators thundered from the arena's main gate, but the first ones came through precisely in time to witness the megabear plow into a line of guards and maul half a dozen of them to death on impact. The spectators spun on their heels to run right back inside, but only managed to crash into the throng behind them, adding to the chaos.

The second wave of escaping prisoners rushed past us, and I spotted all five werebadgers among them. Brukk trotted out behind, burdened with a pile of packs and supplies that I was fairly certain had never belonged to any of us. Sprig had managed to disentangle himself from the fencing little worse for wear, but just as it seemed we were in the clear, Mae dropped to her knees.

"Aaaaaaaaaaaaauuuugh!"

At the same time, the megabear fell to the ground with a great crash, three tongues hanging loose from three open snouts, all six eyes open and staring. Bodies were everywhere— it looked like about half of the guards had survived the battle, and they did not stop firing crossbow bolts into the monster's corpse, even as it lay still.

With a sudden rush of frigid air, black smoke erupted from the corpses of the fallen guards and was drawn to the great bear heap, permeating it. The beast gasped three impossible breaths and howled in triplicate, lurching to its feet and charging straight into the thick of Gluumwilde.

The remaining guards exchanged glances, turned tail, and ran screaming. The flesh of their fallen comrades had been scrubbed clean by the otherworldly black smoke, leaving only bleached white bones showing through their leather uniforms.

"Holy *shit*," Mae said, still on her knees. "Maybe I *am* a necromancer."

NOTES FROM HENK THE BARD:

Another of the most feared creatures in the Conquered Lands: scorpion bats. They're not anywhere near as dangerous as krakens or megabears, but up close they're utterly terrifying.

Lizardfolk gender politics were complex, to say the least.

Anarengu gareech nnnaruelia semmneng translates roughly into "I have faith in you" or "you got this, bro."

The ball of magical energy Frinzil threw at Sprig would have missed him by several feet if it hadn't corrected its own trajectory to connect with its target. Sorcerers, in general, were not a particularly athletic lot, so it was fortunate that most of their spells were not dependent on aim.

CHAPTER TEN

SHORT REST

Mae bolted straight into the wilderness after the megabear. And, I mean, we would have followed her anyway, but the beast was charging roughly in the same direction as the bandit camp, which made it an easy choice. The stampede of escaping gladiators and panicked spectators moved in the opposite direction, for obvious reasons, so our way was clear.

The rest of us hurried to keep up. "Mae! What—" I was trying to wrap my head around what I had just seen and mostly failing. "How did you even do that?"

"You think that had anything to do with me?" She had settled into a brisk walk—so far, it appeared that the bear was sticking to the forest path, which was nice. "The Dark Lord grants all sorts of powers, but I promise you that healing animals isn't one of them."

That bear had been far beyond the reach of simple healing. "Well, if that wasn't you—are we sure we even want to catch up to it? I get that it saved your life—all our lives—but we haven't exactly had the best luck with stuff that have came back from the dead…"

"It's not a zombie," Mae said. "It just—I don't know—stole the souls of the dying lizards or whatever to fix itself up."

It wasn't like I was all that familiar with the practice, but that bear had looked dead to me, and the guards it sucked the flesh right off of certainly were, so if that wasn't necromancy I didn't know what was. Also, we had no way of knowing how permanent the bear's miraculous recovery would be.

"And you're sure it's still—"

"Yes! Ugh! I would *know*!" She stormed ahead up the path.

It was probably for the best, because I needed some time to process everything that had happened. Mae had managed to free us from the gladiatorial arena in a rather spectacular fashion—it was, in fact, the first sign that drunk Frinzil might have been on to something when she recruited a witch instead of a warrior to begin with. There was surely something Mae hadn't said much about the particulars of her escape, but I hoped Brukk could help flesh out the details there. And anyway, the prison break wasn't what was bothering me most.

What was bothering me most was *necromancy*. One zombie squirrel (or even two—I honestly didn't get that good a look at the second one) might be a fluke. The whole business with the carrion crawler infecting the heron was harder to explain, but it could theoretically be chalked up to some gap in my education. But this third instance made it more than just a pattern—I had watched a seemingly dead megabear drain the essence of those lizardpeople and charge off none-the-worse-for wear. I wasn't sure how, but one thing seemed indisputable: Necromancy had absolutely returned to the Conquered Lands.

My mind turned to history. It was the elves who wrested the continent from the lich kings at the dawn of the Fourth

Age, and they took pains to obliterate every last lich. Eight
necromancy-free centuries certainly lent credence to the theory
that they were successful. And necromancy was born in the
Conquered Lands—as far as anybody knew, there had never
been liches anywhere else. But what if one had survived, hidden
deep in the earth somewhere, growing in power for centuries?
If some ancient necromancer had awakened, similar undead
incidents might be unfolding across the countryside. And if
that were the case, it could mean…

Well, it could mean a lot or it could mean almost nothing.
My parents had come over from Westerhelm with their employers,
but the rest of the servants at the manor were mostly muddledfolk like me. And stories had been passed down to them
about life under the goblins before Westerhelm arrived. The
elders who told those stories, in turn, had grown up with tales
of life under the harpies who held dominion before the goblins.
And the general theme was that the language and cuisine might
change, but for the people at the bottom of the pile, one regime
was a lot like another. In practice, would life under an undead
monarch even be that much different from what we had now?

We marched on, breaking occasionally to rest. The bear
kept moving, seemingly with purpose, cutting north into the
wilderness after a couple of hours. Fortunately, a two-ton beast
does not travel easily through dense foliage, and it flattened so
much wildlife that we barely had to slow down after leaving
the path. Sometime past dusk, though, we came to a section
of the forest where new growth had sprung up, possibly after
a wildfire. Which meant the bear could go over the trees rather
than through them, leaving a much less obvious trail.

Soon afterward, Mae announced that our quarry had fallen
still. Not dead, mind you, but lying dormant and impossible to

sense through whatever supernatural bond linked them. I wasn't at all sure of her reasoning, but it was an excuse to finally make camp, which was good enough for me.

Brukk rummaged through his newfound supplies for some travel biscuits and dried meat and distributed them among the group.

"Not that I'm complaining," I said through a mouth full of biscuit once we were settled. "But were travel rations really worth running back into a gladiatorial arena for? After you'd only just escaped?"

"What? No, those were just some bags I found. They're not what I went back for."

We had settled into a pattern where I would speak in common, since Brukk understood it well enough, and he would reply in his native tongue. Sprig was content with getting only half the conversation, and Mae—who was off on her own, sitting cross-legged under a tree—would ignore us regardless, so it seemed to work for everyone. Brukk finished arranging dry wood on the fire and turned to rummage through his new supplies.

"They confiscated the old man's book when they tied me up for transport," he said. Sure enough, Brukk pulled out his mentor's spellbook. He held it open to the first page, which was smeared haphazardly with something dark and caked-on that I hoped wasn't blood.

"What *is* that?"

"I had Sprig show me how to write your name. Now it's inscribed, just like you said, and no one else can read it. It's your spellbook, forever."

I was overwhelmed. If Brukk had truly inherited the book from his mentor, then it was his to bequeath. And spellbooks were often inscribed by the seller (mostly for the aforementioned winner-take-all-wizard-murder-spree reasons—rendering the book useless to anyone but its buyer made delivery a whole lot safer). So, in theory, Brukk could certainly inscribe it to me. Mind you, the splotches he had made were not in any way, shape, or form *my name*, but there was at least a chance his crude attempt had worked. Of course, there was a greater chance that he had unintentionally ruined the most exquisite object I had ever laid eyes on.

I was nevertheless moved by the gesture. "Thank you. Honestly, I... thank you." The intimidating black and white markings that covered Brukk's face were doing nothing to diminish the gentle kindness of his expression. Which made me realize that there wasn't going to be a better time to breach that subject.

"Brukk," I said. "We should talk about those tattoos."

"They're something bad, aren't they? I kind of figured they were something bad."

"I'm pretty sure they mean the summoner you worked for owed a lot of favors to a lot of gods and demons," I said, hoping to ease him into the next part as gently as possible. "And the thing is, now *you* owe those favors."

Brukk turned his eyes to the fire. "So I'll pay them back. Or try to, at least. If that's not enough, what's the worst thing they can do? Kill me? I almost died like five hours ago at the, uh... fighter place." There was no word in orcish for *coliseum*. "I've almost died a whole bunch of times this week."

Now his gaze shifted to some detail on the ground near his feet. "And maybe next time I *will* die, tomorrow or the next day, or the day after that. The job is super dangerous, so you kind of have to be prepared for it. But... I'm sorry, this stuff is hard for me to talk about. It's just that when it does happen, I don't want to die alone."

He raised his eyes to meet mine. "Which is what I wanted to talk to you about. I'm kind of…" He looked away, then met my eyes again.

"I'm kind of, I think, in love."

My entire body flooded with panic. It wasn't that I didn't like Brukk. Brukk was great. But I'd spent my adult life trying to avoid conversations like this one, and now my fight-or-flight response kicked in.

"Pee!" I blurted. "I have to go—"

"Only I don't know how to tell her," Brukk continued earnestly. "And she actually still scares me kind of a lot—I'm worried that if I do it wrong she might, like, set me on fire or something? So I need your help."

Mae! He was in love with Mae! A wave of relief rushed over me, followed instantaneously by confusion. "Wait, you're in love with *Mae?*"

"You didn't see her back there," he said. "The way she bent that monster to her will—she's the strongest, toughest, most beautiful person I've ever met, and I want to spend the rest of my life with her, whether that's a hundred years or just a couple more days."

His sincerity moved me. Also, the fact that he had presented an extravagant gift to me rather than his intended romantic partner (who would have no use for the spellbook but certainly could sell it for a small fortune) either showed admirable strength of character or remarkably poor planning.

"You're a girl," Brukk said, grinning. "So you can tell me what to say to make her like me back."

"Brukk…" I was grasping for the right words. "I don't think

it works that way." In truth, though, I had no idea how it worked. Intimacy, I understood—I sought it in my friendships, even if I wasn't particularly good at cultivating them. But even discussing romantic entanglements usually got me all sweaty and riled up—and not in the good way.

"Look, I know you really like her," I said. "But no matter how much you like someone, you can't win them like a prize."

"But she must want some kind of person," Brukk said, resolute. "Help me figure out what that is, and I'll just be like that."

I sighed. First of all, it wasn't necessarily true that she was sexually attracted to anybody, but as far as I knew I was a freak in that regard, and I had no intention of opening that can of worms. "Think of it this way. Imagine someone you have absolutely no interest in romantically."

"Like a troglodyte. Or a scorpion bat."

Weird example, but okay. "Sure. So imagine a troglodyte you recently met told you they wanted to marry you. How would that make you feel?

Brukk's face fell. "Am I a troglodyte to her?"

"No, that's not what I—ugh." I started over. "Okay, imagine someone who's perfectly lovely, but who you would want to marry as little as you do a troglodyte."

"Like you!" he said.

That was equal parts comforting and offensive, but I pushed ahead. "So if it were me who wanted to marry you, is there any way I could act to make you feel the same way about me?"

He cocked his head, and the look on his face told me he was carefully considering it. Noooooope. *No no no no nope.*

"Brukk, I just can't help you with this," I pleaded. "I'm the worst possible person to talk to about romance stuff."

Sprig, who had only been privy to my half of the conversation, suddenly perked up. "Wait, are we having a sex talk?" He was packing a pipe full of some leaf or root he had found in the woods, and the aroma was… unusual, if not exactly unpleasant. "I'm a great person to talk to about romance stuff."

"Really?" Brukk asked in common. "So how you make scary elf love orc good?"

He took a long pull on his pipe. "Well, that depends. What are your intentions with this scary elf?"

"To make orc bride and love and protect until forever and give many strong orc children."

Sprig walked over to the log Brukk was sitting on, and Brukk shifted to make room. It was not a huge log. "We can work with that," the druid said. "What are your moves? Like, pretend I'm her. Show me what you've got."

"Okay!" Brukk said cheerfully. He took both of Sprig's hands and gazed deeply into his eyes. "How many strong orc children elf want?"

At first, I had been happy to retreat from the conversation, but now it was Sprig's intentions I was worried about. You know what, though? They were both fully grown adults and could make their own decisions about… whatever was happening here. I found a spot across the campsite, where the blaze of the fire between us would give them some degree of privacy without leaving Brukk completely abandoned in case things got weird.

Then I did what I always did when things at the Institute started getting hormonal, which was to bury my head in a book. Fortunately, I had a good one on hand. I opened Brukk's spellbook to the inscription page. The ritual of ownership had two stages, and the part that bequeathed the book from one owner to another had already been completed, theoretically. I took a tiny bottle of ink and a quill from my belt pouch and wrote my name in the center of the page, on top of Brukk's smear. After speaking the incantation of claiming, I held my breath.

Before my eyes, both inscriptions faded, absorbed into the parchment. *It was working.* Of all the schools of magic, sorcery relied the most heavily on ritual and pageantry. And although the physical components, the spoken incantation, and the occasional hand gesture all played their part, at the core of every spell was the written word. A sorcerer's spellbook was a literal repository of magical energy, and when I transcribed a spell, it created a well of power only I could tap.

I could barely keep my hands still (when I got excited, nervous energy tended to channel involuntarily into my wrists and fingers—it wasn't great for spellcasting, but what could you do). I managed to open both of my remaining notebooks—one to Duplicate Tome, which I'd be casting, and the other to the first cantrip I had ever mastered, Magical Stamp. Fortunately, Dupe was an iron nail spell, and unlike dried mistletoe, nails weren't consumed with every use. It also required very little energy from the spellcaster, so I could probably get all the magicfrom my two remaining notebooks into the new spellbook before my strength gave out.

I had spent enough time organizing and categorizing my spells that this part was old hat—I placed the nail in my lap and laid one hand on the Stamp spell and another on the blank spellbook, imagining them to be extensions of my own body. Then I muttered the brief incantation and simply willed the spell to transfer from one book to the other. I felt a gentle tingle as the energy flowed through me—

And bounced right off the fancy new spellbook, giving me almost the exact same jolt of hard, dull pain I felt the time I tried to stick my head through a closed window.

My heart sank. *It had accepted my name, though!* I willed the book to reveal its owner, and the word *Frinzil* materialized on the inscription page, along with Brukk's smear. I could feel the connection as strongly as I could with my notebook, so there didn't seem to be an ownership issue. It was more like the book's enchantment wasn't strong enough to contain the tiny amount of magical energy in a simple cantrip. It couldn't be full of magic already—to start putting spells in it, another sorcerer would have had to claim the book first, which would have prevented me from even getting this far.

Brukk's grand gesture, such as it was, had apparently wrecked the thing.

I wasn't about to give up hope before exhausting every possible avenue, though. If magical storage was truly the issue, I might be able to re-enchant the book myself—I didn't have anywhere near the skill of whoever had crafted it to begin with, but with care, I might be able to cobble together a working spellbook. On a whim, I found the one non-magical book I had with me—a discarded accounting ledger from a village cooper which the bandits hadn't bothered to steal—and repeated the experiment. Sure enough, the columns of numbers on the ledger's first page appeared in the spellbook as intended.

Emboldened, I tried again, and the rest of the book followed. I focused and was able to call any list or table to the first page with a mere thought, which was the kind of feature you'd expect to find in a really fancy—and perfectly functional—spellbook.

Now my mind was racing. Nobody would ever purchase a book this expensive to copy non-magical texts, but since its limitations seemed to be rooted in how much magical energy it could store, and the information I was transferring carried none, its capacity for mundane text would theoretically be infinite. I could visit a library and walk out with every book in the building under my arm.

My train of thought was interrupted by a sharp cry from across the campsite. In the moonlight, I saw Mae scamper to her feet and disappear into the trees.

My first instinct was to alert the others, but Mae's scream was quickly echoed by a low moan coming from the other side of the fire. It was a soft, relaxed, *pleasurable* sound, and I couldn't identify which of my companions had made it, but the absolute last thing I wanted to do was investigate further. So, both out of genuine concern for Mae and an overwhelming desire to be anywhere else, I followed her into the forest.

I didn't have my Irritating Lights spell with me (which in itself wouldn't be the ideal way to light my path, but it was the only illumination spell in my repertoire). And Mae was headed back into the old growth of Gluumwilde, so all I could do was feel my way through the trees and navigate as best I could through scattered patches of moonlight. After a few minutes, Mae called out again in a short grunt, followed by a smattering of curses. Signs of a struggle? I hurried forward into a clearing.

There, bathed in moonlight, was the megabear's motionless form, lying face-up, its torso cut open, its entrails arranged in a crude star pattern across its belly. Mae sat at the point of the star, at the throat of its central head, arms covered to the elbows in blood, ceremonial knife in hand, head thrown back.

"Take it, you cursed bastard!" she howled at the night sky. "I offer this soul to my lord and master, Lrksuul the Thrice-Damned. Choke on it, and give me what's mine! Do you hear me? Here's your fucking tribute, I DEMAND MY REWARD!"

NOTES FROM HENK THE BARD:

Although muddledfolk might not carry physical traits from the various non-human civilizations that had ruled the Conquered Lands, they soaked up culture from just about everyone. A lot of what's considered muddledfolk cuisine, for example, is actually harpy in origin—the extreme methods required to make grubs and worms palatable can turn anything delicious.

If anything, iron nails channeled magic more efficiently with repeated use. Frinzil had done this particular spell so many times that hers already felt like an old friend.

Frinzil's father, who couldn't read, gave her the barrel-making ledger as a gift when she was six, and she invented an elaborate story about its contents rather than break his heart by telling him it wasn't really a "book" book. She always told herself she kept it because the back of each page was blank, and she might use it to take notes. In truth, it was her very first book, and she loved it as much as any that she would ever own (for the record, it also taught her a ton about barrel-making at a very young age.)

MAE

Taryamil was born in the elf warrens within the foothills of Mt. Altoronti, with a powder-blue complexion that was much closer to the pale skin of the high elves who she served than it was to the deep elves of the cavern kingdoms. However, elven society was rigidly organized by class, and the tone of her skin, dictated by so trivial a matter as the altitude of her birth, was a permanent reminder of her station. She watched as her firstborn, Ortonaut, marched steadily from the cradle toward his inevitable life as a soldier or palace guard, without even the hope of anything more to spark his imagination.

When she found that she was to be blessed with a second child, Taryamil couldn't bear the thought of leaving this legacy of hopelessness to a daughter as well.

So she traveled, alone, beyond the elvish domain, to the highest pass on a nearby peak, where A'maelote was born as fair as the summer moon. Taryamil returned to the warrens, where a few years later, her daughter caught the eye of a high elf family precisely as her mother hoped she would. Mae was brought in to wait on their youngest daughter as soon as she was old enough to begin work. The two girls were raised almost as sisters, although Mae understood perfectly well that Selerme's actual sisters couldn't be banished on a whim if they used the wrong tone or forgot to lose a game. Still, it was the best life her mother knew how to give her, and Mae was grateful for it.

Her older brother, alas, hadn't anywhere near as much opportunity and no gratitude to speak of. He did, however, have that particular combination of brashness and stupidity that drove young men to recklessness in every civilization the world has ever birthed. So, rather than reporting for his first day of military duty, he struck out into the forbidden tunnels looking for the deep elves he was certain would welcome him with open arms. It didn't matter that the cavern kingdoms were, if anything, more rigidly organized than their mountainous cousins. Because what he would find in the depths was something else entirely.

When Ortonaut returned to the warrens, he didn't fully understand what he had done. His immortal soul—which, to be fair, he wasn't using for anything to begin with—was promised to the Demon Lord Lrksuul, and he was genuinely proud of whatever absurd errand the Lord's disciples had sent him on, which was clearly only meant to hasten its delivery.

As children, Ortonaut had always been Mae's protector, and she loved her stupid brother probably more than he deserved. So she stole the most expensive-looking object she could find from her employers—an ornate, jewel-encrusted chalice—and made Ortonaut lead her through the tunnels to his new masters to bargain for his freedom.

The Disciples of Lrksuul turned out to be mostly goblins and orcs, along with a pair of troglodytes and one fire spriggan.

As you might imagine, they had no intention of parting with an immortal soul for anything as prosaic as material wealth, and certainly not for something they could just as easily take by force. Mae, however, made considerably more of an impression than her brother had, and they knew a good trade when they saw one. She agreed to enter the service of Lrksuul as a witch, and in return, they would leave Ortonaut out of their plans.

Once she had offered up the souls of one hundred sentient beings, her brother would be released from his debt. It was made explicitly clear that she needn't kill any of them herself, which was a vital component of the agreement—as much as Mae wanted to keep Ortonaut safe, she had no intention of sacrificing a hundred innocent lives to do so. But as long as she was at hand to perform the ritual when someone or something died, Lrksuul would get a soul, and she would get incrementally closer to the day when she would secure her brother's freedom and—theoretically—leave the demon's service as well.

When she returned to her mother's home to make her farewells, however, she found Selerme waiting for her. At first, Mae was sure she would be arrested for theft, but it turned out that no one had even noticed the missing chalice. Selerme simply missed her friend—she had never been made to examine the great imbalance of their relationship, and genuinely thought of Mae as a sister.

Mae knew in her heart that she couldn't stay. The power of Lrksuul was already coursing through her veins, and if she didn't go meet what fate had in store, she was certain it would come to find her. Whatever that fate might be, she wasn't about to risk the safety of either of her families.

Selerme was inconsolable, but gave Mae three small, precious gems as a parting gift. They were the only items of value she possessed that were hers to give, and as sheltered as she was, she knew that they would be of much more use in the unknown wilds of the Conquered Lands than at home in her jewelry box.

It wasn't until that moment that Mae truly understood how much she had sacrificed to save her brother.

And thus, her life as a scavenger of souls began.

NOTES FROM HENK THE BARD

Taryamil: *tarry-AM-ill*

Ortonaut: *OR-ton-ot*

A'maelote: *ah-MAY-loat*, in case you forgot.

Selerme: *Seh-LAYRM.*

Lrksuul: *lurk-SOOL.*

Ortonaut's soul wasn't *literally* immortal, of course, but you needed a cosmology with some long-range upside when you grew up in the elf warrens.

In lieu of a hundred people-souls, Lrksuul would also accept the sacrifice of an even greater number of lower animals—there was a poorly defined conversion system based mostly on weight.

PERCEPTION CHECK

Mae collapsed, her limp body beginning to slide off the massive bear's slick corpse. I threw myself at the mountain of gore in a mostly-futile attempt to slow her descent, worried that she might smack her head on one of the jagged rocks that marked the points of the entrail star. Blood was everywhere. It was not great.

I did manage to cushion her impact with the ground by being mostly underneath her as she reached it, at which point she let out a sharp groan, disentangled herself from me, and bolted toward the campsite. Elves see much better in darkness than humans, so all I could do was to follow hesitantly in her wake. By the time I made it back, Mae was nowhere to be seen.

I did find Brukk snoring loudly by the fire, and Sprig's legs sticking out from underneath a nearby bush. I cleaned up as well as I could (mostly wiping blood off my arms with the robe I was still wearing, which was far from ideal) and found my own spot to settle down. I realized that we hadn't actually discussed any sort of lookout plan—thus far, one night had been spent blackout drunk and the other was just tunneling and jail, so this was the first time the issue had come up. It was just as well that night watch fell to me, though, because I couldn't even imagine sleeping. For hours I stared into the darkness, trying to reconcile everything I had told myself about witchcraft—that it was more or less like any other branch of magic—with the grim, gory spectacle I had witnessed. I had genuinely believed Mae was trying to catch up to the megabear because she wanted to *save* it.

I must have nodded off eventually because I woke myself with a startled snort under the harsh, mid-morning sun. On top of it all, it seemed I was a terrible lookout. I looked around in frantic confusion for signs of trouble, but only found the rest of the party going about their morning business.

Brukk rushed to my side as soon as he saw me stir. "You're up!" he said in orcish. "I really need your—wait, what is all over your clothes?"

I groaned and propped myself up, looking down to see clumps of what must have been dried, desiccated bear intestines stuck to the front of my robe. The real surprise, though, was that any trace of actual blood was missing. Apparently when Lrksuul claimed a soul he took the blood but not the ancillary viscera, which seemed sort of arbitrary.

"It's… fine," I said. Was it, though? The memory of Mae's sacrifice had continued to haunt me in my sleep. I decided that even if I accepted witchcraft in theory, I wouldn't make a habit of witnessing it firsthand. "I followed Mae into the woods last night, and…"

"Mae!" Brukk's eyes lit up. "What did you tell her? Did she say anything about me?"

After the night I'd had, the absolute last thing I wanted was to get into another conversation with Brukk about his prospective love life.

"She did not," I said, more brusquely than I intended to.

"Oh, right. Okay." He fidgeted, avoiding eye contact. "Was that all? Or..."

"Oh!" Brukk said. "No. I, uh... the thing is, last night I was talking to Sprig, and he said I needed confidence. Like, the kind only experience could bring?"

"Oh no—Brukk, did he pressure you into something you weren't comfortable doing?"

"No! It was, like, really comfortable. And I definitely feel more confident now." He cocked his head in thought. "Some of it might not directly apply to, uh, other people. But things went, um, a little further than I thought they were going to? And it was fine! I mean, I learned a lot of stuff. But..."

His expression shifted into a mild panic. "I think I accidentally made Sprig my orc bride."

I sighed. "Did you exchange any vows?" I might not have any experience with courtship rituals, but I knew what a wedding was. "Promise to be committed to each other romantically for the rest of your lives?"

"I don't think so." He paused, considering. "No, definitely not."

"Then you're not married. If all it took was one intimate encounter, half of the Sorcery Institute would be married to, like, three quarters of the Sorcery Institute."

"Oh, thank gods!" Brukk muttered, exhaling.

At that point, Sprig finished dumping an armful of loose dirt on the fire, pointed at Brukk with both hands, and made quick releasing motions with his thumbs as if he were firing tiny crossbows. Brukk legitimately blushed.

"Look, there she is!" Sprig said. I turned to see Mae gathering her things by the tree line. Somehow, her torn cloak and underlying travel clothes were immaculate. "Brukk, go talk to her!"

Brukk looked equal parts nervous and excited. "Do you think I should?"

"No!" I said. "Brukk, just... no. I don't think this is the right time." Mae's expression was stone cold, much like the one she'd worn when I'd first seen her at the Crumpled Buckler. If there was ever going to be a right time for Brukk to put the moves on her (and I could scarcely bring myself to imagine that there would be), it certainly wasn't now.

"Oh, you've for sure got to choose your moment," Sprig said. "Remember what I taught you about—"

"Can we talk about anything else?" I interrupted. Brukk and Sprig seemed to be on the same page about last night's encounter, which hopefully meant things wouldn't get weird between the two of them. Still, the less I was involved, the better.

"Sure," Sprig said. "Actually, before we head out today, I was hoping we could try something. When we were trapped at the arena, you said I was a real druid. And you were right! I made an old wooden gate bloom out of nowhere—who knows what else I can do?"

He squared his shoulders. "I want to try healing your leg."

If there was any chance Sprig could end my throbbing, itchy misery, I was more than willing to let him try. He took a knee, laid both his hands gently on my shin, and concentrated silently with his eyes closed for a solid minute. Alas, the discomfort beneath my ever-filthier bandages continued unabated.

"Ugh—why?" he moaned. "Yesterday, I had so much confidence! I knew I could do magic, and I just did it."

"Sprig, I need to come clean," I said. "I cast something. I shouldn't have done it without your permission, but there's a sorcery spell called Overconfidence, and yesterday at the arena I—"

"Cast it again."

"There's no guarantee it will—"

"Cast it again! If you make me feel the way I felt yesterday, I can do this. I can do *anything*. I'm sure of it!"

My mistletoe reserves were almost depleted, but I was swept up in Sprig's enthusiasm. I managed to conserve a single pinch by going light on my fistful, and the moment I had cast my spell he puffed up his chest, tore my bandages off with far too much vigor, put his hands directly on my wound...

And just kneeled there, grunting and grimacing, as the elation slowly eked out of him and he slipped into the period of extreme self-doubt that inevitably follows Overconfidence. In retrospect, I should have faked it. The line between being confident because you're under a spell and being confident because you think you're under a spell is so fine that I should have simply gone through the motions, saved my mistletoe, and let Sprig generate unwarranted self-assurance all on his own.

"I'm sorry," he said, burying his head in his hands. "I thought maybe this one time I wouldn't be so useless."

"Hey, just because you don't know one particular spell doesn't make you useless." I winced a bit as I said it, since Brukk was now washing my wound with the water he'd boiled the previous night to refill our canteens. At least I was finally getting my bandages changed, and the scabs were mostly stuck to rotting plant matter rather than the bandages themselves, so Sprig barely even tore anything open in his ill-fated attempt at medicine.

"Why don't you take a moment," I said, "commune with… whatever you can commune with, and focus on what you *can* do." If we made good time, we could be at the bandits' hideout in five or six hours, so if Sprig had any hidden reserves, now was the time to find them.

Of course, Sprig wasn't the only wild card on my team when it came to magical abilities. As soon as Brukk finished with my leg, I walked gingerly across the campsite and spotted Mae a short distance into the woods, her back turned to me.

"Mae, we need to talk," I said.

She didn't turn around. "Must we?"

"Look, I know you have this whole air of mystery going on, but this is it. We're marching into the bandits' lair, and they nearly killed us last time. If we're going to pull this off— if we're even going to survive it—I need to know what you can do."

She turned to face me, her cheeks streaked with tears. "Nothing, alright? What I can do is nothing. I swear eternal loyalty to Lrksuul the Thrice-Damned, and the only spell he gives me in return is *Bond With Familiar*. Do you have any idea how much you have to sacrifice to earn a second goddamned witch spell?" Her voice was dripping with disdain. "I'm honestly asking, because I pray to that shit-stained asshole every night for Demonic Fireball, and I was sure last night was finally going to put me over the line."

Bond with Familiar? If the witch version worked anything like the sorcerer equivalent, the bond Mae shared with an animal familiar was sacred. She could see through its eyes. Feel its emotions.

"The bear was your familiar," I said. I couldn't get past it. "And you—you…"

"It wasn't easy! You think it was easy? It felt like sacrificing a *child*. But it's not like I'm the one who killed him!" Mae clenched her eyes to hold back tears. "*I never kill them.*"

Now I understood how she was able to sense the dire heron back at the altar of necromancy—she had been casting out with her senses for an animal companion to bond with. My stomach dropped as I came to a more troubling realization. Mae didn't have any combat magic whatsoever. When the bandits attacked us on the first morning, she hadn't vanished into the woods awaiting orders.

She was simply leaving us to our fates so she could clean up the battlefield.

What had she said was in her contract? *'The immortal souls of any vanquished enemies or collateral damage.'* I was an idiot.

"No, you didn't kill him. But if somebody—if one of us— happened to die all on our own, you'd be ready with your knife, wouldn't you?"

"What? No! I'd never—"

"Oh, I'm not saying it would be easy," I said. I felt betrayed, which made me feel stupid, and I wasn't sure which I liked less. "But it couldn't be harder than *sacrificing a child.*"

Her face hardened. "You know what? You're right. I only signed up because real adventuring parties are basically traveling murder carnivals, and I figured I'd claim the sloppy seconds for Lrksuul. But so far the only casualties have been some large game, my dignity, and your stupid fucking leg." She shot a glance at my bandaged shin. "How's that going, by the way? Infection setting in yet?"

Mae stormed past me, slamming her shoulder into mine as she went. I was no fan of confrontation in general, and I admit that the argument had shaken me. But I had wanted to know what Mae was capable of, and I certainly had my answer. Since I apparently couldn't trust her any farther than I could throw her, that left me with Brukk's and Sprig's limited abilities and whatever spells I could cast with one pinch of mistletoe and an iron nail.

And about five hours to figure something out, because I had a raid to plan.

NOTES FROM HENK THE BARD

Disappearing blood may be unsettling, but it's super convenient if you ever find yourself elbow-deep in ritual sacrifice.

Frinzil's parents hadn't taught her anything about traditional orc marriage rituals, but since Brukk and Sprig hadn't spent an entire month building a secret, majestic wooden monument and then set it ablaze to represent the intimate bond that was theirs alone and not for anyone else to behold, he was safe on that front, too.

The supplies Brukk had pilfered from the arena included not only a pot for boiling water, but also a very nice linen shirt that was perfect for bandaging. It was quite the haul.

FORCED MARCH

We broke camp and headed north (the trip downriver had taken us much further south than we needed to go, and we'd essentially been backtracking since our escape from the arena). All morning, a periodic, high-pitched trilling noise from somewhere in the woods had been assaulting my concentration—I hoped we'd leave it behind once we set out, but whatever kind of creature was making the sound, the forest was apparently thick with them. If anything the calls became even more frequent as we hiked. It was far from ideal, since I needed all the focus I could muster. My companions, it turned out, had very little help to offer on the raid-planning front.

"I don't know what the problem is," Sprig said. "I can draw magic from the forest—like, I can feel it swelling up inside me. But I can't seem to do anything with it. Here, watch." He stopped and put both hands around the trunk of a cedar sapling and closed his eyes, clenching pretty much his entire face in concentration. "Grow, damn you! Ugh! I did this with an old gate yesterday! Shouldn't an actual living thing be even easier?"

"Easier, maybe," I said, "but if it's a different spell, it's a different spell." I tried to remember everything I'd learned about druidism in Comparative Magic (which wasn't a ton, but without access to the Institute's library, it was the best I could do). "What about a totem? Druids usually adopt an animal or plant or even a specific kind of rock to help them focus their magic. Do you have anything like that?"

"Hmm." He paused to consider it as we resumed our hike. "Could hallucinogenic mushrooms be a totem?"

They could be, I supposed, and to be honest it would explain a lot. At least Sprig was more confident about his directions than his spellcraft. "Oh, it's definitely this way," he said as I pulled out my map to help me visualize our progress. "I've been to their camp twice, and the second time I got super lost on the way back, so I had to memorize every single landmark. Like, you see that tree right there?"

He gestured toward roughly ten thousand indistinguishable trees.

"I *totally* recognize that tree. It's this way for sure."

By then, I knew better than to rely entirely on Sprig's sense of direction. But the entire venture hinged on finding the bandits where he said they'd be, so that ship had more or less already sailed. His memory of the bandit camp itself seemed fairly sound, so we focused on logistics. The lair was a burrow dug into the root system of a massive willow tree, with the entrance obscured by hanging branches. The interior wasn't large, even by ratling standards, which was fine by me—I intended to get in and out as quickly as possible.

The only question was how many bandits would be actively trying to stop us. And, of course, exactly how we would deal with them—to be honest, I was getting cold sweats just thinking about that part. Sprig certainly didn't seem like he would be much use in a fight, and I wasn't ready to revisit the subject with Mae. In fact, I half expected her to disappear after the morning's confrontation, but she marched along at the front of the pack, setting a brisk pace for the rest of us.

As brisk as possible, at any rate. We had left the new forest growth and were now plunging deeper into the thick of Gluumwilde, which slowed our progress considerably. As we attempted to navigate a particularly thorny section of brambles, the physical discomfort must have shown on my face.

Brukk winced empathetically. "Your wound looked like it was healing at least some," he said in orcish. "How does it feel?"

"Honestly? It itches like a *love of mothers*." I had one precious pinch of mistletoe left, and casting Resist Itch was the absolute last thing I was going to do with it.

"It hurts like a what?" Sprig asked. He looked genuinely baffled.

"A love of mothers. It's from an orcish word. There isn't really a literal translation."

"Yeah," he said. "I don't think that's what that word means."

"It is!" I insisted. "*Kurgegraskuk*—my dad used to say it all the time. It's like, when something is as intense and powerful as the love of one's mother."

Brukk looked like he was trying to stifle a giggle and losing the battle. "Kurgegraskuk mean 'motherfucker,'" he said in common, through a wide grin.

I was in shock. How much had I been swearing all these years without even knowing it? How much did *my dad* swear? My mysterious woodland nemesis trilled again, and I remembered that I had significantly more urgent matters to worry about.

"Okay, Brukk," I said. "What's the biggest, meanest thing you can summon? Not a chipmunk and not a wolverine."

Brukk swallowed hard. He pulled several squares of stained burlap out of his pockets and rifled through them—I remembered seeing them back in the werebadger pit, but I still didn't know what they were. "There," he said at last, holding up one of the torn pieces of cloth so I could see it. It was completely covered on one side with black smudges.

"Um, what am I looking at?"

"Oh!" He turned the square over to inspect the front. "This is just how I remind myself how the Old Man made the circles. See how big this part is?" I couldn't differentiate between sections of smudge, but realized that if I had the components to cast Eyes of the Orc, I would be able to see the subtle variations in texture as clearly as Brukk did.

"That means the circle was pretty big," he continued. "And this part is extra rough because I remember how frustrated I was with the details of the border inscription."

I was dumbfounded. "Brukk, who taught you to do this?"

"What? I just kind of made it up—did I do it wrong? I know I ruined a perfectly good burlap sack…"

"This is writing. You've invented an *orcish written language*."

"No, it's just markings I make to help me remember stuff."

"That's what writing is!" Even if it wasn't completely developed yet, he had created a system that used texture and emotional cues instead of the symbols his eyes weren't equipped to decipher properly. "You need to teach me this," I said. "We can teach it to other orcs! You could—"

"Hey," Mae's voice came from somewhere in the thicket ahead of us. It was the first time she'd spoken since our altercation that morning, and her inflection betrayed no hint of emotion. "There's a trail up here."

I still hadn't made my peace with the whole Mae situation. I had thought we were becoming friends, which was clearly not the case, but was I just letting my hurt feelings get the best of me? Mae had never explicitly claimed to have combat magic. She certainly let us believe that she did, though, so if we met our end relying on skills she never had, that was at least getting close to murder-betrayal territory. Was I completely out of line to feel somewhat murder-betrayed?

We pushed through the foliage, and sure enough, found Mae waiting on a forest path. It was narrow and not well-tread, but it had plainly been cleared by someone or something. And it lead in the exact direction we needed to travel. After a solid hour of increasingly dense woods, it felt too good to be true.

"This isn't a trap, is it?" I wondered aloud. "Don't some faeries create magically convenient paths to lure hapless travelers to their doom?" The untamed wilderness of the Conquered Lands was legendarily dangerous, and as far as travelers went, we were about as hapless as they came. The more I thought about it, we'd been incredibly fortunate on the deadly forest front—most of our troubles had come in the form of other people rather than wild animals. Then again, other than that initial stretch, our forest travel had been largely on the heels of a rampaging megabear, which surely had done a lot to keep predators at bay.

"Gluumwilde isn't a faerie forest," Sprig said. "I *live* out here. You can't just *live* in a faerie forest. Have you ever met a faerie?"

I hadn't, and based on his reaction, now I wasn't sure I wanted to.

"Wait," Sprig said. His eyes grew wide, and he looked even more frightened than when I mentioned faeries. "I know exactly what this is. They make their own trails, to get from ambush to ambush. This is a *bandit* path."

A bandit path. Our chances of being re-ambushed on route to our counter-ambush had just risen exponentially.

"Do we leave the trail?" Brukk asked. "Do we hide nearby, wait for them to come to us, and ambush the ambushers?" The shrill, repetitive call of the unseen woodland creature cut through the quiet, but now it sounded both irritating and ominous.

Kr-kr-kreeeee. Kr-kr-kreeeee.

It was really getting under my skin. "What even is that thing?"

"Purplebird, I think," Sprig said.

"What the hell is a purplebird?" Mae asked. It seemed she was finally concerned—or at least irritated— enough to join the conversation.

"Oh, I don't know if it has a real name," he said. "I mean, I assume it does. But it's, like, purple? And it's a bird?"

I didn't quite manage to suppress a groan. Whatever the creature was, it had us all on edge. As far as the bandit trail went, however, the truth was that our adversaries certainly knew the woods around their own hideout better than we did. Our best chance to catch them off guard was to reach their lair as quickly as possible, which meant taking the trail.

It was tense going. We made a counter-re-ambush contingency plan: Brukk would drop to summon at the first sign of trouble. I would keep my last, precious pinch of mistletoe between my fingers and a notebook open to Cause Minor Wounds. Mae would keep a lookout for a potential new familiar, hopefully finding something ahead of any trouble. And Sprig would... see if the attackers had anything wooden he could sprout? It wasn't much, but at least they would have one less weapon to use against us, if at least one of their weapons happened to be made of wood.

Every shadow was suspect, and every random noise had us jumping practically out of our skins. But panic bred efficiency, and we made good time. As we marched, though, the too-familiar trilling became more and more frequent. *Kr-kr-kr-kreeeee.* It was starting to sound sort of *raspy* to me, almost as if it weren't a bird at all, but something imitating a bird.

Kr-kr-kr-kree! Kr-kr-kr-kreeeeeeeee!

One of the calls came from behind us, and the other from above.

"That not purple bird!" Brukk squealed in common. "It *ratling* bird!" He fell to his knees and started frantically outlining shapes on the ground. A third call came from directly in front of us, and a dark shape burst onto the path.

By the time I could make out the graceful form and violet plumage of the apparently-majestic purplebird, my spell was already cast. The bird gave a startled squawk and flapped haphazardly into the canopy, three feathers from its wing twirling gently to the ground.

My last pinch of mistletoe was gone. Whatever was waiting for us at the bandit hideout, I was going to have to face it without magic.

NOTES FROM HENK THE BARD

To be fair, Frinzil's last pinch of mistletoe wasn't going to be that much use against a band of cutthroat ratlings anyway. But still.

Technically, their misfortunes so far hadn't been *entirely* from the civilized world, since there had been that whole business early on with the zombie dire heron. But they could only blame themselves for that one.

CHAPTER THIRTEEN

THREATENED AREA

By mid-afternoon, we had arrived. The bandit trail became wider and more well-tread as we traveled it, and ended abruptly at an enormous willow tree with branches that fell so low they completely obscured whatever might be beneath them. It was exactly as Sprig had described it.

Except for one detail: laying on the ground at the end of the path was a massive rodent the size of a pony, complete with a harness and a saddlebag hanging from one side. The towering, twisted trees flanking the willow grew so close together that they made a veritable wall of vegetation. There was no getting around it.

"Ugh," Sprig said in a half-whisper. We were all crouched in the foliage just off the path. "I didn't think that thing was, like, a permanent guard."

I had never seen anything like it before. "What even is it?"

"It's a capyboros. Pretty much like a capybara, only bigger."

"Uh-huh. And what's a capybara?" The very first thing I was going to do when I got back to school was check out some books on regional flora and fauna.

"Sort of a combination between a rat and a dog? They're super relaxed and gentle."

"Okay, so it's not dangerous."

"No, capy*baras*, I mean. Capy*boroses* are mean as hell," Sprig said. "I thought it was going to bite my face off last time, so I just kind of dropped the girls' things and ran."

The beast's eyes were open, but it lay still on the ground with its tongue hanging out of its mouth, lightly panting.

"Is it… *sick*?" Brukk asked.

"Okay, new plan," Mae said. "We kill the horse rat, sacrifice its soul to the almighty Lrksuul, I get my Demonic Fireball, and this whole day gets a hell of a lot easier."

I shot her a dark look. Even if I had been eager to witness another demonic sacrifice—which I most assuredly was not— I would still prefer not to deal with our bandit problem by setting the whole gang of them on fire. I mean, as angry as I was about both my orb and my leg, the bandits could have just as easily put that arrow through my neck. Leaving us alive after their ambush was surely a conscious choice, and if there was any way we could retrieve our possessions that didn't involve mass murder, I was certainly hoping to try that first.

I closed my eyes, reaching out with my senses, and was instantly rewarded for the effort. The magical stamp spell I had cast days ago was still active, and it lit my mind up like a beacon. "The orb is close by!" I said. "*Very* close."

"I told you!" Sprig said, pleased. "Their hideout is tiny."

"Can you just bond with the capyboros, Mae?" I asked. "And make it your familiar?"

"Not while it's sleeping. Or… whatever it's doing. I already tried."

"But if we wake it up first—"

"Look," Mae said. Her stare was vaguely threatening, but her voice trembled. "It might be a problem with the rat, or I might have just burned out my familiar thing for a while." She looked away. "The last one took a lot out of me."

I wasn't sure what to do with a Mae who was being open and communicative, but the point relevant to our immediate predicament was that, other than demonic sacrifice, she had nothing. With no spell components other than my iron nail, I also had nothing. It was already well established that Sprig had nothing. Which left Brukk. I had finally had my raid plan, more or less through the process of elimination.

My party looked at me expectantly (well, Brukk and Sprig did, anyway—Mae was staring at the ground).

"The only thing we've done in three entire days that's been even moderately effective," I said, "was to send something big and scary ahead of us and follow its path of destruction. So we're going to do that again. That's the plan."

"Great," Mae said. "But you get that I can't just pull a megabear out of my ass, right?"

"Not you," I said. "Brukk, we never finished our conversation back in the thicket. About the biggest, scariest, meanest thing you can summon?

Brukk nodded solemnly and took the smudgy burlap square out of his bag, holding it up, again, as if it could possibly mean anything to me.

"It's a dungeon dog," he said. "I think. I mean, I'm almost positive."

It turned out the reason Brukk mostly knew summoning circles for small mammals was that if a situation called for anything bigger, he was usually hiding too far away to observe the ritual. Dungeon Dogs were big, hairless things shaped roughly like canines but with a mass of rubbery tentacles instead of a face. They were often found scavenging monster corpses left behind in dark, remote locations. His mentor had summoned them regularly, but Brukk had never seen it done until the very end.

"The day I finally worked up the courage to watch from up close..." He looked at the ground. "That kraken came out of nowhere They're attracted to magic—it must have sensed the summoning ritual. He never got to finish, but I saw him make the circle. I got my notes."

He set his jaw. "I can do this," he said. "I'll summon the beast, and control it. You can count on me."

"I know I can."

We had been speaking in orcish, so I translated the plan for Sprig and Mae. "Brukk is going to summon a dungeon dog. What we're going for is controlled chaos—if our monster fights their monster, great. If their monster just lays there unconscious, we send ours straight into the bandits' den. Either way, we create the biggest distraction possible so we can grab the orb and run."

"They keep the really good treasure in a big pile by the door!" Sprig said. "This could totally work!"

Mae stood in silence for a moment. "I don't actually know what a dungeon dog is," she said at last, "but if he can't make friends with it, maybe I can. As a backup. Just in case."

Brukk appeared unshaken by her lack of confidence. "You should all stand back," he said in orcish. "*Way* back."

He stepped out of the bushes and onto the path. Then he made a long gash in his palm with his knife, bent over, and got to work drawing a massive circle on the trampled, uneven forest floor. His eyes were closed, and I realized that he couldn't properly see the symbols he was making anyway. He was working entirely from the *memory of his mentor's movements*.

In less than a minute he finished, out of breath, and dove out of the circle as the ground beneath him exploded in a cloud of sulfur.

A shriek pierced the air from inside the smoke, which quickly cleared to reveal the writhing form of something at least five times the size of a dungeon dog. It had a powerful beak that could snap tree trunks in two and twelve massive tentacles covered with skin as rough as bark. Its six eyes burned with mindless rage.

Brukk had summoned a tree kraken. He fainted immediately.

The capyboros lifted its head and took one look at the tentacled horror emerging from the sudden, unexpected cloud of smoke. It made a sound halfway between a whistle and a chirp that somehow managed to perfectly convey abject terror. Then it bolted under the branches of the willow, and the kraken launched itself after it, tearing out entire chunks of tree in the process.

Mae was wide-eyed and utterly frazzled, as if she had gazed into an endless abyss and found only madness and despair gazing back.

"Yeah," she said. "It did not want to be friends."

NOTES FROM HENK THE BARD

In the thousand years since dragons disappeared from the Conquered Lands, krakens had moved in to occupy their place in the ecosystem as apex predators. They evolved quickly and magically, their descendants moving from the oceans into the forests, mountains, skies, and anywhere else dragons had ever ruled. No matter what form they contorted themselves into over the centuries, however, krakens were not dragons. They were birthed in a much deeper, older realm, and their thoughts were nothing at all like what you might find inside the skulls of anything native to the surface world. When confronted with the scrambled, otherworldly horror of the kraken's mind, Mae had the sense to disengage immediately, but Brukk hadn't. His brain simply shut itself down as a safety mechanism. Which, granted, was a good way for his brain to get itself eaten by a tree kraken, but that was still probably better than the alternative.

The fact that Frinzil recoiled from the thought of setting her tormentors on fire proved that she was A) a genuinely kind human being, and B) an absolutely terrible adventurer.

Most capyboroses are, in fact, just as genial as their smaller cousins. But this one was trained to sense fear, and Sprig, on the heels of a fairly ugly breakup with multiple ratlings, had not been his best self on that particular day.

Since so much of the Conquered Lands' economy under Westerhelm rule was plunder-based, adventurers were everywhere, leaving carcasses in remote locations all over the continent. Needless to say, dungeon dogs were thriving. The situation was certainly not ideal if the heritage of your displaced ancestors was buried under some secluded temple somewhere, but if you were a dungeon dog you were living your best life, for sure.

CHASE COMPLICATIONS

In a panic, I tried to remember everything I knew about tree krakens. It wasn't a lot. They were only considered the fourth or fifth most dangerous species of kraken, but to put that in context, that also made them the fourth or fifth most dangerous creature in all of the Conquered Lands. Their sheer bulk, strength, and ferocity were bad enough, but the worst part was their flame—krakenfire only burned living matter, passing magically through inanimate objects, which made it impossible to shield against. They could burn you to cinders from the other side of a stone wall. I had cringed at the idea of Mae tossing a Demonic Fireball into the bandit den, but this... This was so much worse.

Something was tugging at my senses. I focused on my magical stamp and felt the orb retreating rapidly. Creeping forward cautiously, I peered through the gap in the willow tree's mangled branches.

There was no entrance to a secluded burrow. Only a wide-open dirt path that led into a huge forest clearing, where poorly constructed wooden buildings were piled on top of each other. Trees had been planted—decades ago, judging from their height—to form a nearly-solid wall around the settlement, with boards nailed to the inside perimeter to cover the gaps. The kraken was chasing the capyboros toward the center of town, and ratlings were running in terror everywhere I looked.

This was no hidden ratling bandit den. This was an whole hidden ratling city.

"But… that's not…" Sprig trailed off, then turned to look at me, utterly aghast. "Did I hook up with *two entirely different sets of identical triplets?*"

According to my spell, the orb was still on the move—as a matter of fact, it was tracking with the movements of the capyboros.

"It has the orb!" I said. "Somehow, the capyboros has the orb!"

"Aaaaauuuuuugh!" There was frustration in Mae's groan, but mostly she sounded resigned. "Okay, fine," she said. "You were right. I thought that if I joined some stupid band of stupid adventurers who were going to get themselves killed anyway, I could finally sacrifice some actual people instead of small forest creatures. But then you *were* people, and you cared about each other, and you cared about me…"

Without finishing her sentence, Mae bolted, heading into the ratling city at a full run. "Wait here!" she shouted without turning around. "I'll bond with the rat and get your glow ball thing back!"

"No! You said that you couldn't—"

"Also, if we went with my plan we'd be finished and gone already," she yelled, now out of sight completely. "I'M JUST SAYING."

Love of mothers. "Sprig, stay with Brukk!" I said, launching myself into a sprint after Mae. The very first thing they teach in Adventuring 101 is not to split the party, but with one of my people unconscious and another hurtling toward danger, that ship had sailed. I darted under the willow tree and was met by a dozen panicked ratlings trying to get out the way I was coming in. They scattered—I was twice their size, and they probably assumed I had come with the giant, tentacled horror.

Which, to be fair, I kind of did.

The scene was unmitigated chaos—ratlings were diving into ramshackle houses, climbing the trees of the city wall—there were *hundreds* of them. A wave of guilt crashed over me. This was an entire community. I had unleashed an uncontrollable death machine not just on the bandits who had attacked us, but on innocent people. One way or another, I would have to do more here than just fetch my orb and leave them to the kraken.

Mae was a short distance ahead of me. Past her, I saw the capyboros just barely dodge the kraken's lunge, spin on its heels, and plunge into a narrow space between two buildings near the center of town. Everything here was built ratling-scale, so the wooden structures packed seven or eight stories into forty feet of height. The kraken skittered as if deciding whether to squeeze into an alley that was much too small for it or simply burn the capyboros out.

If it chose the flame, would that solve my problem for me? The capyboros would burn to ashes, but its saddlebag would be untouched. The problem was, for all my research, I still didn't know exactly what a hunter spirit was, much less whether it counted as "living matter" for krakenfire purposes.

Before I had to find out, two crews of dauntless ratlings leaped out of shacks on either side of the alley and hurled heavy rope nets over the kraken. For the briefest moment, I thought they might immobilize it long enough to attack with their spears. With a flurry of tentacles, though, the monster tore through a section of netting and threw one ratling a good fifteen feet into the air. Then it grasped uneven handholds jutting out from the rickety building—which creaked and swayed ominously under its weight—and started to climb.

Someone barked an order, and the ratling guards—after helping their flying colleague to his feet, I was relieved to see—disappeared around the far side of the towers between the smaller houses that surrounded it.

Mae ran straight into the alley after her quarry. I followed, snatching up one of the ratlings' discarded nets on my way. It might be useless against the kraken, but we were hunting something significantly less horrifying.

Calling the space between the haphazardly-constructed buildings an "alley" was perhaps a bit of a stretch, but the uneven gap was wide enough to accommodate us, and stretched probably a hundred feet to the other side. I finally caught up with Mae, who had stopped to catch her breath, about halfway through. The capyboros was nowhere to be seen.

"Damn you, rat, sit still and let me befriend you." She turned to me. "And what part of 'wait here I'll be right back' don't *you* understand?"

"You are literally not the boss of me," I said through my own panting. "Also—"

A ghastly screech cut me off from the far end of the alley. The capyboros appeared, bolting toward us at a full gallop. It nearly filled the narrow alleyway, so there was no getting out of its way, and no avenue of escape. On a positive note, it did save me from trying to figure out how to say 'I forgive you for sort of trying to get me murdered.' At least, for the moment.

Mae threw her head back, her pupils going white. "Get behind me!" She planted her feet and balled both hands into fists.

The capyboros didn't even slow down.

"Duck!" she screamed just as the creature was upon us. I threw myself to the ground, and the capyboros, remarkably light on its massive claws, skittered right over me without so much as tearing my robe.

Mae, however, didn't make it through the trampling as unscathed. She yelped in pain as I helped her to her feet, her right arm bent in a way I didn't think it was supposed to bend. "I tried to bond," she said, "but all I sensed was blind panic and... a really bad stomach ache?"

A shadow passed over us, and I looked up to see a mass of tentacles in the open space above, temporarily blocking out the sun.

The capyboros must have fled through the alley only to find its pursuer waiting at the other end, then bolted back the way it came. It reminded me of some of the other servants' kids growing up—they were largely awful, I'm not going to lie—trapping mice in the manor basement for kicks. The poor mice would run back and forth, in and out of the same hiding spots over and over until they were finally caught.

There was no reason to think a horse-sized rodent would behave exactly like its tiny cousins, but there was also no reason to think it *wouldn't*.

"Help me string up the net!" I said. "If it comes back through, we'll catch it!"

"Where did you get a—" Mae stopped herself. "You know what, I don't even care." We hastily began affixing the net to the buildings' walls, although with one good arm Mae could only help so much. Architecture didn't seem to be the ratlings' chief strength, and most of their construction materials seemed to be long-dead tree branches and scavenged pieces of wood, so there were plenty of rough edges to secure the netting to.

We hadn't quite finished the job to my satisfaction when we heard a scuffle behind us, on the *wrong side* of the net we had been painstakingly securing. Somehow, the big rodent had made it around the building and was charging at us from behind. Aaagh—that wasn't how the basement mice did it at all. It might well get caught in our trap, but it was going to have to plow right through us—again—to do it.

With no time to think, I threw myself on the ground, which had worked for me the first time. Mae made the opposite choice, leaping into the netting in an attempt to climb over it before the capyboros was upon us.

She was not even remotely successful. The beast thundered over me and hit the net at full speed. The knots we had worked so hard to tie barely even slowed it down and, now tangled up in netting, it somehow managed to panic even more. It skidded to a halt and began to scramble frantically up the side of the building, dragging Mae—at this point just as entangled as the rodent was—right along with it.

About ten feet up, the capyboros wriggled itself free, leaving the net—and Mae—hanging precariously on an outcropping of scavenged wood.

"Aagh, my arm!" Mae cried. "I'm—ow! I'm fine, mostly," Her good arm was very much twisted up in netting, and as she attempted to draw her knife with the other one, it slipped from her grip and fell. Above her, the capyboros finished its climb to the top of the building…

And found a screeching mass of tentacled fury waiting for it. The kraken seized its prey and was immediately beak-deep in capyboros torso. In its death throes, the rodent managed to writhe free, plummeting back into the crack between buildings, missing Mae by a couple of feet, and hitting the ground directly in front of me with a bloody thud.

I screamed. It was completely involuntary and, I think, entirely warranted. I shook off the momentary panic quickly, though, and saw that the capyboros landed saddlebag-side up. Which was a huge stroke of luck because it was quite dead, and there was absolutely no way I could have turned the thing over.

Alas, my frantic rummaging through the saddlebag revealed nothing. It was empty. I closed my eyes to sense the magical stamp—it was right there! So close I should be able to touch it!

Ugh. "I think the orb is in the rat's stomach!"

"Of course it is," Mae deadpanned from above.

As little as I wanted to dig through giant rodent stomach contents, there was little else to be done. I grimaced, grabbed Mae's knife from the ground where it had fallen, and plunged it into the wide gash in the capyboros' belly. At least the kraken had done most of the hard work as far as carving went. I began hacking at a thick, soft membrane that I hoped was a stomach lining. The smell was overwhelmingly foul.

My fingers found something hard and smooth, but it wasn't the orb. I pulled it from the carcass and managed to wipe off enough stomach goo to identify it as one of the sealed jars of spell components from my pack. Going back in, using my magical senses as a guide, I came up with two more jars and—

A large mass of partially digested burlap. It was the remains of my pack. I kept digging madly through the corpse, but the orb was nowhere to be found.

Wait. I had cast Magical Stamp on my bag, not any of the specific items inside it. This whole time, I hadn't been sensing the orb, but the bag itself.

The tree kraken let out a frustrated, ghoulish screech, and I felt like joining in. It was bloodied from its encounters with the ratling guards, which I could only hope worked out better for them than it had for the poor capyboros. The kraken tested the wooden structure beneath it and found some give. With a half-dozen tentacles, it ripped right through the top story of both buildings, raining splintered chunks of wood into the alley.

"It still wants its dinner!" Mae said. There were three short, ratling-height stories between her and the kraken, and two more to the ground. "Get my knife!"

I grabbed the blood-slick ceremonial dagger from the ground where I'd dropped it, but there was no way I could reach Mae before the kraken did, much less free her in time.

"Now cut out the rat's entrails, and arrange them into a star!" With a crash, more splinters rained down. "Quick! It's our only chance!"

I gritted my teeth and went back into the corpse, grasping a handful of intestines and yanking out as much as I could. "Which direction does the point go?"

"It doesn't matter where the fucking point goes! Lrksuul! Thrice-Damned lord of all suffering, ruler of the nether regions of eternal burning! I offer you this soul!"

I finished making what could charitably be described as a star precisely as Mae completed her speech, and the part of my mind I'd been using to track the magical stamp abruptly caught fire. I felt the capyboros' life energy burrow down into the earth. A column of blue light, much like the one that had engulfed Brukk back in the werebadger pit but less dramatic in the mid-day sun, erupted from the ground directly underneath Mae.

The kraken screeched and tore through another layer of shack, but Mae responded with a deep chuckle that chilled me to my bones. "Okay asswipe, let's see how you like this one." With her wounded arm, she held her hand out and screamed two words at the top of her lungs with equal parts triumph and rage.

"Demonic fireball!"

The kraken shrieked as the gashes in its hide from innumerable spear strikes sealed up, and a chipped piece of beak magically filled back in. In the blink of an eye, it was healed completely, the perfect picture of vigor and health.

"Son of a *bitch*," Mae said.

NOTES FROM HENK THE BARD

In a land as vast and incompletely-explored as the Conquered Lands, hidden cities were a popular way to avoid both conflict and taxation, and you can hardly blame ratlings for wanting in on that action.

The ratlings may not have been great architects, but the fact that they kept adding stories year after year without collapsing the buildings was a testament to their architectural enthusiasm, at the very least.

You'll be pleased to know that the guards had fared reasonably well against the kraken. Not spectacularly well, mind you, but they had been as careful as it was possible to be while attempting to subdue a mindless horror and had thus far managed to hold their own.

Not long after Frinzil left for school, the rat-trapping children came face to face with a sabretooth terror-ferret that had burrowed through cracks in the foundation to feed on the mouse population. It isn't important to our story at all, but it did make them seriously reconsider their life choices.

CHAPTER FIFTEEN

SAVING THROW

Rough tentacles, still slick with ichor from wounds that were suddenly mended, tore through the final, ramshackle floor between Mae and what she must have assumed was her doom. I tried to find purchase on the walls to climb, but a thick coating of rodent guts made it impossible (the capyboros' blood was already beginning to dissipate into the netherworld, but apparently Lrksuul had no need of stomach bile or partially-digested foodstuffs).

Even if I hadn't lost most of my books and components, I couldn't think of a single spell that would be of any use. It was happening so fast! One glance upward revealed Mae desperately trying to free herself from the netting, but the next was all eyes, beak, and tentacles. A limp body slipped through the writhing appendages and fell, hitting the capyboros carcass with a wet thud.

I was utterly stupefied when I realized that it wasn't Mae. It was Brukk. How was it *Brukk?* Did Mae's new monster healing spell also somehow involve swotching places with random, unconscious nearby friends?

Witch magic made no sense to me at all.

My shock was quickly replaced by terror, though—he had fallen on the capyboros. Which was the kraken's lunch. I didn't even know if Brukk was alive, but I pushed that thought to the back of my mind, rushed to him, and grabbed an arm and a leg. With one great heave, I managed to slide him off of the slick rodent carcass—how was helping unconscious people off giant animal corpses something I had to do twice within twenty-four hours?—but once his mass had settled on the ground, he was too heavy to drag. I let out a prolonged grunt and pulled with every ounce of my strength, but only managed to move him inches. The kraken tore through one last chunk of building above us, finally within grasp of its prey.

It curled a tentacle around the discarded mass of burlap that I had extracted from the dead animal's stomach, tossed it into its open maw, and shrieked.

Krakens were attracted to magic, Brukk had said. It must have sensed my magical beacon—this entire time, it wasn't after the rat itself, but the enchanted burlap in its stomach. Six great, malevolent eyes stared at me. The beast had gotten what it came for, and now with a single breath, it could burn us out of existence entirely.

Instead, it turned skyward and began pulling itself out of the tunnel it had dug between the two buildings, causing me to wonder—not complain, mind you—why it let us live. Did it simply have more important things to do? Was it drawn to some other bit of magic nearby?

Like, for example, an ancient hunter spirit?

I closed my eyes and reached out with my senses. I had originally cast the spell on my pack, but was there any chance it had also marked the items inside it? If the faintest whiff of magic had settled on the spirit orb, I might be able to—

With a soft moan, Brukk shifted in my arms. What was I doing? How far was I going to take this? I wanted more than anything to go back to the Sorcery Institute—I ached for the library more and more every hour I spent away from it, every night I spent sleeping on dirt, or the damp wooden floor of a prison boat. But did I want it badly enough to get myself killed? Could I live with myself if my obsession led to the death of my friends?

Brukk shuddered and pulled himself up to a sitting position. "Aaagh. That was no squirrel brain. It was more like a thousand squirrel brains? If they were all angry and vicious and desperate to feed upon, like, other squirrel brains?"

"Brukk!" I threw my arms around him in a great big hug —we were both covered in rodent innards already so I might as well. "How did you get here?"

"Oh, I woke up pretty quick and we followed you into town," he said, hugging me right back. "Sprig made friends with a rat lady who lives here. She let us in her house!"

"They yanked me into the building just before the thing could eat me." I looked up to see Mae slowly descending a lumpy mass of tangled net with Sprigg's help. Above them, a ratling peered through the hole that used to be her apartment wall and waved.

"Then your genius friend there tried to save you by mind-controlling his nightmare beast again," Mae continued, "and did not get a different result. Tell me you got the stupid orb, at least."

"I did not get the stupid orb. Forget the stupid orb. The new plan is just to get out of here alive." I paused. "And maybe stop that thing from wrecking any more buildings? Or killing anybody? If we can?"

"Did it breathe fire yet?" Brukk asked. "That's how they killed the other one—krakens only have one shot! Once it burned up the old man, they said it wouldn't be able to make fire again for a couple hours."

"Not yet, as far as I know." I had no idea how to lure a savage beast into breathing fire at me without being burned to a crisp, but hopefully we could come up with something. "Okay, so once it's expended its flame, then what?"

"We chop off all its tentacles," he said, "rendering it helpless."

I looked up at the kraken as it cleared the top of the building and lurched out of sight, limbs wriggling mightily, each one as thick as a sapling. Then I looked at Mae's little ceremonial knife, which I had dropped over near the rodent corpse.

"Cutting off its limbs may not be an option." What else could we even do, though? I remembered the three jars of spell components that I had recovered from the capyboros' innards, located them on the ground, and wiped off as much goo as I could with my robe. The first was ragweed seed, the second was firefly paste, and the third was...

Heck yeah. *Dried mistletoe.*

"We'll lure it out!" I said. "It was chasing the capyboros because it sensed my spell, and my pack was—it's actually a whole thing. But I can slap a magical stamp on pretty much anything. We can make kraken bait!" There was no shortage of shredded lumber scattered throughout the alley, thanks to the beast's rampage. I began collecting scraps of wood, only to be shouldered aside by Brukk, even though he still looked shaken from his ordeal.

"If there's one thing I know," he said, "It's carrying armfuls of stuff."

We hurried to the alley's exit and found the guards battling the kraken directly between us and the town gate. Things did not appear to be going well. I had hoped to get outside the city walls before enchanting kindling, but the best-laid plans often go awry, and this plan was not even laid particularly well. I took a hunk of wood from Brukk, pinched a bit of dried mistletoe from its still-disgusting container, flipped open a notebook, and spoke the incantation.

The moment I cast the spell, the kraken shrieked and turned away from its tormentors, fixing its assorted gazes on me. I hurled the stamped wood with all my strength in a direction that would lead the monster away from us as well as the ratling guards.

It flew all of about twelve feet, hit the dirt, and tumbled about another foot and a half.

"Okay, that went a lot farther in my imagination. Run!"

Just as I had hoped, the kraken made a beeline for the wood, and we managed to clear the immediate vicinity before getting caught in its charge. We kept running toward the willow tree that marked the city gate on a slightly indirect course to avoid a direct encounter with the bewildered-looking guards. Best-laid or not, the plan was working! Still running, I took another pinch of mistletoe to enchant a second piece of wood. This one was going to be rough. Casting the same spell again before my spellbook could recharge meant every bit of magical energy had to come from me, and I had no idea how many times I could even try it before—

"Attaaaaaaaaaaaaaack!"

A volley of arrows flew from somewhere high in the trees that formed the city wall, followed by two dozen ratlings swinging down on ropes. Wait—were these reinforcements, or…

"Rat City for Ratlandiaaaaaaaaaa!"

NOTES FROM HENK THE BARD

Sprigg's new friend was named Rikti. She was a beekeeper. They had only just met, but was there some immediate spark between them that neither could deny, even though they were from different worlds? Maybe!

Frinzil focused on the dried mistletoe, since she needed it to cast most of the spells she still had access to, but finding firefly paste back meant Eyes of the Orc was also BACK ON THE TABLE, BABY.

"Rat City for Ratlandia" doesn't even make sense, logically or grammatically.

CRITICAL FAIL

They were the same bandits who had waylaid us on the outskirts of Dredgehaven. I was sure of it. And the city guards were visibly relieved to see the bandits attacking the kraken instead of joining alongside it—there were clearly some inter-ratling politics going on here that we weren't privy to.

The initial volley of bandit arrows carried a web of netting that appeared sturdier than the guards' attempt at restraint, binding the kraken to the structure behind it. It was a promising development, but this entire fiasco was my responsibility, and I still intended to do my part. I finished marking the second piece of wood—the beast had already devoured the first one—my knees buckling with the effort. That energy drain hit me like a punch to the gut. Brukk steadied me, then took the decoy from my hands and threw it toward the monster with far greater force than I would have managed.

The kraken ignored it entirely. In fact, it appeared to be tunnel-visioned on one particular bandit, a deft archer who had thus far managed to dodge every strike of tentacle and beak. It was as if the beast smelled something on her that it craved more than a chunk of magically stamped kindling.

I had a pretty good guess what that was. "It wants the orb!" I shouted at the bandits. "The glowing thing you stole from us a few days ago!" I didn't want any people to get killed fighting this thing—even bandit people. Although if some of them got wounded I would probably be okay with it.

The archer flipped backward away from the fight, fired an arrow with a line attached high into the trees of the city wall, and swung up into the canopy. She emerged a moment later to rejoin the fray, lighter by the weight of one ratling-sized backpack.

The kraken didn't seem to be singling her out from the pack any longer. Instead, its attention now returned again and again to the tree line.

"So it's in the tree, right?" Mae said flatly. "The stupid orb is in the tree?"

The tree in question was boarded up with planks high into its upper reaches, filling the gap between it and the next tree over. Brukk jumped and managed to catch a handhold on one of the boards.

"Forget the stupid orb!" I said. For the record, I still desperately wanted the stupid orb. "It's not worth dying over!"

"I don't know," Brukk said in orcish, continuing his ascent. "I'm a pretty good climber."

Sprig rushed to the tree. "Brukk, wait!" he said, then turned to me. "What did he say?"

"Brukk okayest climbing!" he yelled down helpfully.

Sprig slapped both hands against the lowest board and closed his eyes in concentration. "You know what? I'm fairly okayish climbing too." On command, every plank nailed to the tree sprouted, from bottom to top, and Sprig hopped from upward-growing branch to upward-growing branch, passing a very surprised Brukk entirely and settling into a steady climb about halfway up.

Even at half-scale, Rat City had quite respectable walls, with old growth and nailed-on additions stretching a good sixty feet up. Sprig hadn't been boasting about his climbing adequacy and made quick progress, with Brukk following close behind. Meanwhile, ratling-on-kraken violence raged on. The monster had freed itself, and its eyes were now fixed on the same patch of treetop as our own.

Unfortunately, another pair of eyes was watching that spot as well. The bandits must have left a lookout, because a weighted cord was flung out from somewhere in the trees, wrapping around Sprig and tangling him up in the branches.

"We've been made!" Sprig shouted. "I'm—*gack.*" One loop of the cord had wrapped loosely around his neck. "I'm stuck here pretty good!"

"Hold tight!" Brukk said in orcish. "I'm right behind you!"

"I don't know what that means, but I'm okay!" He insisted. "Just get the orb!"

I exchanged a glance with Mae, who gestured weakly at her limp right arm. "Yeah, I'll go ahead and guard the escape route," she said.

I threw myself into the newly-sprouted foliage. I was a decent climber myself, but even so, I was only about halfway to Sprig when the second bolo flew. This one was for Brukk, and a lead weight hit him square in the forehead on its third orbit around him. If he hadn't already been pinned to the tree by the bolo's leather strap, he might have fallen out of it entirely.

"I'm fine!" he said. He said something else as well, but the second remark was obscured by a particularly angry kraken wail that sounded way too close. I redoubled my efforts and soon caught up to Sprig, then Brukk, both of whom assured me they would have themselves free in a jiffy, and that I should definitely go on without them.

"But watch out for leather cords!" Sprig called out from below me.

It was solid advice. I had been scanning the nearby treescape as I climbed and spotted our attacker just as he readied a third bolo. I locked one elbow around a branch, whipped open a notebook, and grabbed a pinch of mistletoe from my pouch.

Cause Minor Wound wasn't the most impressive spell, but it *was* unexpected. And when a painful scratch materialized on the bandit's throwing hand as he was about to release bolo number three, the surprise must have thrown him off balance. Not only did the leather cord go tumbling straight into the tree's lower branches, but the bandit lost his footing and promptly followed it.

He let out a shrill, piercing whistle as he fell, which I appreciated because the sound let me know that his fall ended a short way down into the foliage, and not after a deadly, 60-foot drop. I was far less pleased a moment later when I learned that whistle wasn't simply an expression of shock or fear.

It was the signal to his boss that something had gone wrong.

The arrow struck me not just in the same leg that was pierced three days before, but the exact same spot. I screamed as my shin exploded in a pain that was familiar in its general contours, if not this particular intensity. I managed to hang on to my branch, but there was no way I was doing any more climbing anytime soon. Up or down.

It certainly didn't feel like one at the moment, but that turned out to be a blessing. Below me, the kraken was also confronting the bandits and having an experience not unlike my own. Its scream, however, came with a blinding column of magical green fire, and if I had managed to climb even a few feet up from the spot where I was pinned, the blaze would have enveloped me.

Krakenfire, up close, was something that I was not at all prepared for. There was no heat whatsoever, but the sight of it burned my eyes. There was no way to know if the kraken had aimed for the orb intentionally, or struck it via dumb luck. But every bit of life around the ratling's bag, barely two yards out of my reach, was incinerated instantly. The top of the tree, severed cleanly, went crashing down outside the city walls.

As if time had slowed, I saw the backpack topple end-over-end through flakes of green ash, and the orb tumble out from inside it. It was still glowing, which meant that whatever the hunter spirit was, it wasn't "alive" enough to be harmed by krakenfire. I wish I could report that I had snatched it out of the air, but I would have been in no condition for such athletics even if the orb's trajectory had carried it within my grasp.

All I could do was watch it fall.

Sprig and Brukk were gawking at the devastation above me—I don't think they even knew the orb was plummeting. And Mae clearly heard it before she saw it. The sound that drew her attention, of course, was shattering glass.

The hunter spirit, freed from its prison after nine centuries, shot off like an arrow to the city wall, then over it and off toward the distant horizon.

NOTES FROM HENK THE BARD

Okay, this is going to take a bit of explaining because Frinzil never did learn the whole story. But here's the deal: The bandits' history with Rat City was long and full of drama. When they spotted Frinzil's group on the trail near by, they first planned a quick re-ambush on the hapless travelers who had restocked supplies. But when they learned where Frinzil was headed, they plotted to use her as a distraction to mount a raid on the city itself. Having already assessed the party's strengths, the bandits figured the group would need some help to make any kind of a ruckus. So half of them rushed ahead to pre-poison the gate guard (with some tainted grain stuffed into a sack full of junk they'd been hauling around for three days). The other half stayed behind to taunt the party with bird noises, just for fun. The bandits were as surprised by the kraken as anyone, and although they enjoyed sitting back and watching the ensuing chaos, they finally stepped in while there was still something left of town worth looting.

For the record, the bandit triplets recognized Sprigg but bore him no ill will since their tryst meant more to him than it did to them. They worked in a burrow hidden under a willow tree bit lived in a city hidden behind a different willow tree. Ratlings hide a lot of stuff with willow trees, it turns out.

Frinzil is actually downplaying her climbing skills here. Half her childhood was spent crawling through ventilation shafts to get in and out of the manor's forbidden library. She could climb like nobody's business.

The bandit watching the treetops had, like, an entire sack full of bolos. He had been left in charge of protecting some unknown object in a bag, and damn it, he took that responsibility seriously.

The arrow that hit Frinzil's leg, incidentally, was fired by the exact same archer as the first time, who knew exactly what she was doing and, frankly, was just plain mean.

EPILOGUE

The kraken flung itself over the city wall and followed. I watched as it swung away through the trees, chasing the point of light that had already faded in the distance.

The bandits settled into a prolonged confrontation with the city's defenses, and both sides ignored us completely. Which was fortunate, since it took Brukk and Sprig a solid twenty minutes to get me out of that tree. The arrow in my leg made walking impossible, so once we were on firm ground, Brukk carried me out the willow gate on his back. No one tried to stop us. We ventured a short distance into the forest until we could no longer hear the sounds of fighting.

And then stopped because, in all honesty, none of us had any particular place to go. Mae tried her new spell on me, but it did nothing whatsoever—it turned out to be Heal Animal, which only worked on creatures incapable of rational thought. Brukk got to work bandaging, a process that was dramatically more painful than it had been the last two times. My leg was messed up good.

My spirits were, if anything, in even worse shape. Without the hunter spirit, I could never return to the

Sorcery Institute. Well, perhaps if I brought them something much more valuable—like the ancient scroll—but all hope of that had shattered alongside the orb. That scroll had remained hidden for centuries—an extremely talented scoundrel who knew what she was looking for might be able to find it, but we didn't even have a cut-rate spellcaster pretending to be a scoundrel.

Which was a shame. Because once it cleared the city wall, the hunter spirit had shot off in the exact direction of the Temple of Unrelenting Evil. The scroll was still there. And the temple was only half a day's travel to the east, at most.

My team was still grasping at straws. "Why not hire our own scoundrel?" Sprig asked. "The scary elf can't be the only one in Dredgehaven."

"No time," Brukk said in common. "Plus, new scoundrel steal quest same as old scoundrel. That scoundrel's whole job."

"So we find the temple and lay in wait," Mae offered. "We let them find the scroll, and take it from them."

The color drained from Brukk's face. "No, no, no. They kill us. They kill us bad."

"It's, fine" Sprig said, although the disappointment in his tone suggested otherwise. "We'll figure something else out. Some other way to make a bunch of money that's not, like, impossible."

Even from the pit of hopelessness, hearing Sprig say that word aloud triggered my mother's voice in my head. *Things are only impossible until you decide that they aren't.* It was true that all I had managed to do since setting foot in the Crumpled Buckler three days before was to dig myself deeper and deeper into a hole. But there was a way out, provided I was willing to dig a little deeper still.

"The orb is gone forever," I said, "but the quest only dies here if we let it." In my heart, I knew I hadn't hit rock bottom yet.

"Because I know where we can get another one."

NOTES FROM HENK THE BARD

Mae was about to quip that "creatures incapable of rational thought" meant the spell would definitely work on Frinzil, but ultimately decided it wasn't the time.

Also, Mae was the first demon worshipper in recorded history ever to be granted Heal Animal. Lrksuul the Thrice-Damned was basically an asshole, and one with a sense of humor, which is even worse.

AUTHOR'S NOTE

Thank you, first and foremost, to all the people who read various versions of this book as it meandered towards publication and helped shape it in ways both large and small. Rose Lerner, to begin with. Also Rose Lerner, Rose Lerner, and Rose Lerner. Caroline Dombrowski, for reading a fairly recent draft in its entirety, as well as several chapters of a much earlier one. Geoff Gill, whose kindness I definitely took advantage of. Beth Meacham for critique and encouragement on the first chapter of that very first draft, as well as the whole gang in my Cascade Writers group, including Raven Oak, Coral Moore, and a whole mess of other folks whose names I've unfortunately forgotten because it was way back in like 2016 and I am terrible. Mindi Welton-Mitchell, not for reading it as much as just listening to me gripe about it week after week in our little Ballard writing group. Scott Gable, for being an always-reliable sounding board and bottomless well of support.

And Dawn Marie Pares. Always Dawn Marie Pares. You're the entire reason that I get to do any of this, and I love you more than cheesy words in a goofy author's note can ever convey.

Thanks also to Nintendo Cheesefries, who no longer wants me to address him by anything other than his given name (which is neither Nintendo nor Cheesefries) because he is almost seven and apparently nicknames are for babies? You should all know that while I've been working on *Spellmonkeys book one: Tavern Rats* and *Spellmonkeys book two: Dungeon Dogs*, Cheesefries has been busy writing *Spellmonkeys book three: Firewing Cats*. He's a solid 5,000 words into it and so far there's a lot of stream-of-consciousness stuff about cooking and Animal Crossing and lists of zip codes he likes. Needless to say, it is SPECTACULAR.

Thanks to everyone who read this book a chapter at a time on Kindle Vella, which was a weird (and ultimately kind of dumb) experiment. And to Frost Llamzon for the gorgeous portrait of Frinzil for the Vella marketing page (it also graces the back cover, so I guess SUCK IT to the poor saps who bought the ebook).

Also, finally, thanks to the anonymous editors at Tor who were so gushing in their rejection letter for an earlier, novella-length draft of *Tavern Rats* that I almost made you all wait another two years to read it while I shopped it around to other publishers.

You know what, though? Screw it. The book's ready. *I'm* ready.

Spellmonkeys has gone through a lot over the years. It was initially conceived as the fourth book in my Chooseomatic series, and there's still a ton of really goofy humor in it from those days. (The whole thing with krakens replacing dragons in the ecosystem, for example, came about because it was going to be called *Advanced Krakens and Catacombs* and I was trying to justify the title.) As it evolved, of course, I became more and more invested in the storytelling aspects. Frinzil and the gang started to feel like real people. The Conquered Lands started to feel like a real place. And I'm not going to lie, I spent a fair amount of time fretting about tone inconsistencies. But at the end of the day, I finally came to realize that any issues in that regard are feature, not a bug.

This book is who I am as a writer. The silliness and trope-skewering of the Chooseomatics. The banter and frantic action of Conspracy Friends. The wry observation and raw, unapologetic *feelings* of Arabella Grimsbro. It even has a little bit of that Robot the Robot thing where I take a tiny part of myself that I've always been afraid to show the world and just stick it on a page and pretend I'm talking about someone else.

I've always beenmagnificently bad at writing to market, and the more I tried to make Spellmonkeys conform more closely to what I thought fantasy was supposed to be, the less I liked it. Because all I can do is write a book that *I* love, and hope some of you will love it, too. Not all of you—I mean, my career is so all-over-the-place that every single thing I've written has fans who tell me it's one of their all-time favorites but don't really care about anything else I've done. So if Spellmonkeys is that book for you, the one thing I've written that really hits home, then congratulations: you're the same kind of nerd as me. *I see you.* And I'm immensely grateful that you're out there reading this book. Which I know ends on a bit of a cliffhanger, but don't worry! I specifically waited to publish it until part two was finished, so you can read the rest of it right now (or at the very least in a few short weeks if you devoured this, like, the very moment came out).

If you want to stay in the loop about future releases, please sign up for my author newsletter at youmgmark.com. (If you do, I'll also send you a free short story about Frinzil's first encounter with magic when she was thirteen. It's pretty great!)

I have more to say about Spellmonkeys (and even a few more people to thank), but I've got a whole other author's note to write for book two, so we should save some for that.

Thank you, again, for reading. It means more to me than you could possibly know.

—*Matt*

MATT YOUNGMARK

SPELLMONKEYS
BOOK ONE: *Tavern Rats*
BOOK TWO: *Dungeon Dogs*

ARABELLA GRIMSBRO
Arabella Grimsbro and the "Wonderful" Wizard
Arabella Grimsbro, Warlord of Mars
Arabella Grimsbro Twenty Thousand Leagues Below

CHOOSEOMATIC BOOKS
Zombocalypse Now
Thrusts of Justice
Time Travel Dinosaur
U, Robot (A CHOOSEOMATIC MINI)

CONSPIRACY FRIENDS
Clandestine Maneuvers in the Dark
The Weird Turn Pro
Hot Vatican Nights

FOR EARLY READERS
Robot the Robot is Here to Help

WWW.YOUNGMARK.COM

Made in the USA
Columbia, SC
28 February 2022

56982738R00112